• • • •

Steel City Seven

THEY CAME FOR OUR GUNS, THEY CAME FOR OUR FREEDOM

*The Continuing Adventures of
Sam Budda and Nick Savarese*

• • •

William Lafferty

New Image Press, Pittsburgh, PA

New Image Press
4433 Howley Street
Pittsburgh, PA 15224

FIRST EDITION DECEMBER 2009

ISBN 978-0-9842963-0-9

• • • •

This book is dedicated

To the intrepid gun enthusiasts

Of the United States

Who have stood their ground

Against those who would disarm them

And render them defenseless

Against crime and renegade governments

• • • •

· · · ·

Personal Acknowledgements

I would like to thank my wife, Cathy, who has been patient and encouraging through readings, re-readings, revisions and discussions that must have seemed endless.

I am indebted also to my editor and friend, Drew Nelson, a true master of the written word, who patiently worked with my tortured prose to the point of making some of it readable.

Any errors in the text are my own.

· · ·

THEY CAME FOR OUR GUNS,
THEY CAME FOR OUR FREEDOM

Prologue

The right to "keep and bear arms" as provided for in the Second Amendment to the United States Constitution, has been interpreted recently by the United States Supreme Court in District of Columbia et al v. Heller , 554 U.S. ____, (2008), to mean that a citizen has the Constitutional right to possess a firearm in his home for self-defense, although that right is subject to reasonable regulation by the government.

Critics of firearms ownership ask "Self-defense against what?" The most immediate threat is, of course, criminal attack. But there is another threat as well. That threat is attack by an out-of-control government. The Declaration of Independence states: "whenever any form of government becomes destructive of these ends [supporting the basic rights of man] it is the right of the people to alter or to abolish it, and to institute new government, laying its foundation on such principles and organizing its powers in such form, as to them shall seem most likely to effect their safety and happiness."

In sum, our founding fathers envisioned that the government might become oppressive and that we would rebel, with violence if necessary, against tyranny. Many people find this a ridiculous notion since they cannot conceive of our government as an oppressor, and even if it were an oppressor, they cannot conceive of opposing the government with individually owned small arms. That small bands of armed citizens are not likely to prevail against the United States Army does not negate the viability of armed resistance, however, for even the government will be loath to become so oppressive that it must subdue individuals with massive force, and ultimately face twenty million armed and outraged citizens. And as for the likelihood that the government will become an oppressor, it was only seventy years ago that people all over Europe reasoned that Hitler would stop after he invaded one or two countries.

But Hitler did not stop, and instead created one of the most oppressive regimes of modern times. He and the Nazi party identified German Jews as enemies of the state, confiscated their property, uprooted them from their homes, and herded them into cattle cars so packed with bodies that many of them died standing up, unable to breathe, and soiled by their own filth. Those who did not die on the trains were transported to concentration camps where they were either worked to death or starved to death or exterminated. Their bodies were incinerated or buried in pits dug by bulldozers. Some prisoners were made to stand in groups naked at the edge of pits and then shot, their bodies tumbling into the void and tangling helplessly with other bodies already there and still others that would follow.

And lest this example be thought to be an aberration, consider the killings under Stalin, probably exceeding 17,000,000, in the 1930's and 1940's; the killing fields of Cambodia under the Khmer Rouge in the 1970's; the ethic-cleansing murders of Bosnia in the 1980's; and the mass murders in Rwanda in 1994. It is not as if we are unfamiliar with the potential of governments to be murderous or that these events occurred so long ago that they are irrelevant to modern life.

The threat of an oppressive government is alive and well. In fact, it was only a few months ago that police, armed with M16 rifles, pointed them at ordinary citizens in New Orleans following Hurricane Katrina, demanding the surrender of all firearms. People were stopped at gunpoint in their boats, in their cars, and rousted out in their houses. Police strong-armed anyone who had a firearm to turn it over, without receipt, to them. This police-state-action was finally stopped by a court, but not before thousands of guns had been stolen by the police, most of them never to be returned. Bear in mind that this disarming of the people was carried out when the police were, by their own admission, unable to protect the population against looters and violent criminals.

The threat posed by crime speaks for itself. Our culture is permeated with deadly crime, organized and unorganized. It is fueled by greed and the desire for power in the criminal underworld. Ordinary citizens have been shot down in car-jackings, robberies, kidnappings, rapes, home invasions, extortions, and at random by some teenage fool performing his gang initiation rite.

Those who oppose the use of deadly force in countering violent crimes believe that the average person could not defend himself with a gun in a criminal attack and that calling the police is a better alternative. Those in opposition counter that they would rather have the chance to defend themselves than submit quietly to their own murder. As for the police, even law enforcement officials acknowledge that they arrive only after the crime has been committed. The police investigate crime; they do not prevent it.

Gun owners are adamant about gun rights not only because they rely on guns as tools for self-defense, but also because many gun owners are part of an enduring tradition of gun ownership that stems from an earlier time when the population was not so concentrated in urban areas. This gun-owning tradition is, in fact, a culture in its own right-a gun-culture. Grandfathers in this culture teach their grandchildren to shoot, take them hunting, and buy them the traditional first single-shot rifle or shotgun. Annual gatherings at the hunting camp are social occasions featuring wide-eyed youngsters listening to the tales of the old men over steaming bowls of chili, huge sandwiches and freshly made pies.

But the gun culture is not merely multi-generational and oriented to hunting. It also a culture that is full of enthusiasm for firearms in general, including the building of custom guns, experimentation with loads for accuracy and lethality, and the development of all sorts of tools relevant to this enthusiasm, such as computer programs for ballistics, devices for measuring range and the speed of bullets, testing media, devices for the support of guns for long range shooting, ammunition loading tools, innovative reactive targets, powders, bullets and primers that perform different tasks, wildcat calibers, precision made sights and triggers, and a written lore having to do with big game hunting, the building and use of firearms, and firearms as used in war.

The anti-gun culture, on the other hand, knows nothing of this tradition or this culture, and sees instead only the rash of killings in most urban settings associated with crime and gang activity. The rationale of the anti-gun culture is simply that if there were no guns, there would be no gun violence. Lives would be saved.

The pro-gun people are impatient with the notion of giving up their rights because other people don't know how to behave. The pro-gun people argue that guns cannot be banned in the face of the constitutional right to own firearms. They argue that if the population is disarmed, it will be as vulnerable to an overreaching government as the Jews were to the Nazis. And they argue that if the firearms of the gun culture were destroyed, criminals would retain their guns, and gun violence would be even worse, as it has proven to be most recently in Australia, where more than half a million guns were destroyed and crime went up dramatically.

The single most important factor that has caused the political left to demand an end to private firearms ownership is that the underclass has, over the last fifty years, expanded exponentially in numbers, bringing with it an exponential increase in crime. Many of these criminals come from families without fathers and the absence of fathers has caused large numbers of children to join gangs as a substitute for parenting not available at home. Not being content with having created the problem, the left now seeks to empower this underclass and to protect it from itself. This protection, in part, takes the form of seizing firearms from the middle class, who might otherwise use them to respond to the criminal acts of the underclass.

Gun owners do not feel the need to protect the underclass from firearms used defensively against criminal conduct. In fact, gun owners cannot grasp why the underclass should have been encouraged to expand its numbers, and they cannot understand why criminal conduct is not met with extreme violence rather than counseling, special programs and the disarming of potential victims.

Politicians in the United States who favor gun confiscation in any of its many forms are up against not merely a fringe population of gun-nut rednecks, but millions of people who insist on defending themselves against crime as well as government oppression, and a gun culture as old as this country with adherents in every part of the nation and in every aspect of American life.

The story that follows involves the killing of officers in the various police agencies of the United States who are engaged in a government plan to seize privately owned guns. The story is not written to condone the killing of police officers, but to raise the possibility that if compromises are not reached, this undesirable result may occur. Tyranny begets violence and police, innocent themselves, are likely to be used as the expendable tools of a tyrannical government. Anti-gun politicians need to understand that the roots of gun ownership are deep, not shallow, and that if they propose to uproot gun ownership, they will have their work cut out for them.

1

Four o'clock in the morning. Twenty-two black clad figures shuffled in formation down Merrimac Avenue of "Century Estates" in suburban Pittsburgh. Silent except for the soft tramping of rubber-soled boots and the rustling of the uniform-fabric, the helmeted black shapes moved past parked cars , an overturned tricycle, past bushes and lamp posts and a plastic wrapped newspaper left over from the day before. At the edge of the Mulhaney lot, the leader held up a gloved hand and stopped the formation. At a hand signal, the figures moved in single file around the sides and back of the house. Six approached the front door, the visors on their helmets down and glistening like the eyes of insects.

Two invaders positioned the arms of a hydraulic jack against the door jam and attached a chain to the heavy door handle. Four more circled the door with rifles shouldered. Once the hydraulic jack was in position, it easily pulled the handle and lock mechanism out of the sturdy walnut door, leaving a ragged hole. The bolts of the lock were still in place however, so the man running the jack clamped a twelve inch bar to the chair, then threaded the chain through the hole in the door. This time, when the jack was activated, there was a ripping, splintering noise as the door was torn from the frame. When the chain was removed from the door, a riflemen kicked the door into the living room, and the intruders, activating powerful lights on their rifles, swarmed into the house.

Clyde Mulhaney was a sound sleeper, but he heard the door being torn from the jamb. He was on his feet and reaching for his robe when the bedroom door burst open. White light blinded him and men were yelling. Mulhaney was too confused to understand. The lights rushed at him and something hit him in the face. As he fell to the floor, he realized the voices were yelling, "Get down. Don't move. Get down."

Mulhaney lay on the floor in complete disorientation, half-conscious, with a broken jaw and a concussion, as his wife, Judy, sat up in bed and stared in terrified confusion at the men who were pointing rifles and lights at her and her husband.

Judy began screaming, "Who are you? What do you want? What have you done to my husband? Get out of here." As her voice began to rise, her sense of outrage began to rise also. She threw off the covers, jumped out of bed and grabbed the muzzle of the closest rifle. She pushed it aside and attacked the rifleman, taking him by surprise and knocking him down. As he hit the floor with the woman on top of him, he fired a burst from his M16 into the ceiling and into two of his colleagues. Another helmeted intruder pulled the woman off his fallen colleague and knocked her out with a butt stroke to her head.

Other invaders carried three squirming, screaming, crying boys into the room and threw them on the bed. The boys immediately fled to their fallen mother. Streaming blood, Mulhaney crawled instinctively to the other side of the bed, next to his wife. The boys hugged him and begged him not to die.

Other men in black ripped the back door off its hinges and occupied the ground floor of the house. Lights now blazed in every room of the house and intruders flooded into the basement as well. Two thugs remained in the bedroom with M4 rifles pointed at the fallen parents and the terrified boys, who clung to their parents as if to life rafts in an ocean filled with terrors.

A shout came up from the basement as one of the men seized an AR15 rifle that lay partially disassembled on a workbench. He dropped the rifle into a large canvas bag held by another uniformed invader. A third man worked on a gun safe in the corner with an acetylene torch. When the lock mechanism clanged to the floor, a sizzling mass of hot metal, he opened the door and extracted several handguns, rifles, and boxes of ammunition. It all went into the canvas bag.

As the bag man went upstairs to collect any other contraband, intruders were pulling down the duct work of the heating system and tearing apart the washer and dryer.

Upstairs, the bathrooms were ransacked. Toilets were smashed and wrenched from their mounts. Medicine cabinets were pried from the walls, leaving gaping holes of plaster and lath. The kitchen was piled high with contents of the cabinets thrown onto the floor. Even the refrigerator had been tipped onto the floor. Pans, silver, dishes, glasses, broken glass, flour, rice, canned foods, frozen dinners, and rolls of paper towels lay strewn. The kitchen faucet was ripped from the sink and a stream of water shot toward the ceiling like a geyser.

In the rest of the house, every piece of upholstering was slit open, lamps were smashed, books and the contents of cabinets were dumped onto the floor, and clothes were torn from closets and cabinets.

The black-suited assailants left as suddenly as they had appeared. Seven year old Timothy Mulhaney called 911 and told the operator that some men had killed his mom and dad. The police arrived with an ambulance. The boys were taken into temporary protective care and the parents were taken to Allegheny General Hospital.

When Mulhaney was finally cognizant, the police explained to him that they were powerless to act, because the invaders were officers of the Bureau of Alcohol, Tobacco, Firearms and Explosives. They invaded Mulhaney's home on a tip he possessed an illegal machine gun, which they had seized and were holding.

"The best thing you can do," the police officer advised, "is get yourself a good lawyer, cause you're looking at a $10,000 fine and twenty years in jail."

2

Clyde Mulhaney was a thirty-eight year old veteran of the Gulf War. He served in the National Guard, was the father of three boys, and worked as an electrician at the University of Pittsburgh. He was a practicing Presbyterian, and he, his wife, and the three boys attended church and Sunday school on a regular basis. It was how he grew up. He was a classic example of the clean-cut American male.

Clyde was raised in Somerset, a small town thirty miles from Pittsburgh, in the thick of one of Pennsylvania's many deer hunting enclaves. From the time he was six, Clyde had gone hunting with his father and uncles and had grown up with rifles and handguns as an ordinary part of life. Now, with a family of his own, he no longer had the time to go hunting, but he kept a small gun collection and he planned to introduce his sons to shooting with the .22 single shot rifle his father had used to teach him.

His wife Judy worked part-time as a nurse, but with three boys, she couldn't manage more than that. The boys needed her at home and if she had worked full time, most of her earnings would go to childcare expenses. With Clyde's overtime and Judy's earnings, they just managed to pay the bills and have a little extra for the occasional restaurant meal and a few new clothes for the boys. When Clyde's overtime was cut, he began to look for ways to reduce expenses and raise money. Finally, he was forced to sell one of his three AR15 rifles. He liked the AR15 because it was the civilian version of the M16 he had been issued in Iraq, and he was well trained with of the gun. The main difference between the AR15 and the M16 was that the civilian AR15 was semi-automatic and the M16 was select-fire, it could be fired either as a semi-auto or as a fully automatic weapon.

One of Clyde's co-workers mentioned at lunch one day that he was looking for an AR 15, and Clyde said he had one for sale. He told his friend that he could take the gun to his gun club and test fire it. That weekend, Clyde's friend fired nearly 1,000 rounds through it, testing for accuracy and reliability. The gun passed all of the tests, and Clyde's friend was about to leave the gun club, but he decided to load one last magazine.

He took careful aim and squeezed the trigger, but instead of a single round being fired, two rounds fired and a third jammed the bolt open. The unfired round was lodged half in and half out of the gun. The shooter removed his ear protectors and looked at the gun in puzzlement.

A club member on the bench next to him said, "Is that a full auto weapon? You know, full auto weapons aren't allowed at the club."

Clyde's friend said, "No. It's not full auto. It's semi-auto, but it seems to have malfunctioned. There's something wrong with it."

"Well," the other shooter said, "you'd better not shoot it any more."

"I'll take it back to my friend and ask him to get it fixed. Do you know Clyde Mulhaney?"

"Mulhaney. Yeah. He's a member. And that's his gun, huh?"

"Yeah, I was thinking of buying it, but he'll have to have it looked at first."

Clyde never had a chance to have it looked at. He disassembled the gun that night to see whether there was anything obvious that might cause the gun to go full auto, but he couldn't see anything. It looked normal. Puzzled, he left the gun disassembled on his workbench until he could take it to a gunsmith later in the week. But that was not to be. Two days later, before he took the gun in for repair, the federal government invaded his home.

After Clyde and Judy were released from the hospital, they went to pick up their boys. Child and Youth Services, refused to return the children to a non-functional household with parents who might be criminals. Desperate, Clyde and Judy went to the office of a lawyer nearby and begged for help. Jay Silver, took their case and three days later had their children back. Clyde, Judy and some neighbors had returned their house to a semblance of normality. But as the children returned home, Jay Silver told Clyde he should prepare himself for other problems.

He was right. Three weeks later, Clyde was charged with possession of an unlicensed machine gun and attempt to transfer an unlicensed machine gun. Each count carried the penalty of a $10,000 fine and ten years in federal prison. Silver continued to represent Clyde and sought help and advice from the National Gun Rights Group. The NGRG politely refused on the grounds that they couldn't risk being seen as supporting people with unlicensed machine guns.

The Pennsylvania Sportsman's League, did offer support, however, as did friends and neighbors. Both Jay Silver and the lawyer for the Sportsman's League believed the case was a clear example of police overreaching and that winning it was a slam-dunk. And besides that, the Sportsman's League attorney pointed out, the case may not even come to trial because it seemed unlikely that the US Attorney would approve the prosecution. In all probability, the charges would be withdrawn.

BATF and other police agencies had done stuff like this before. Usually, it happened during appropriations hearings when they made the case for more money and manpower to control rampant crime. After the infusion of several million dollars, ordinary police sergeants became "SWAT Commanders" and ordinary police departments became paramilitary organizations.

But the attorney for the Sportsman's League was wrong. The US Attorney approved the prosecution. Both the Sportsman's League attorney and Jay Silver were alarmed. The first line of protection against police impropriety, prosecutorial discretion, had failed. The only remaining lines of protection were the right to a jury trial and the court itself, which has the power to dismiss the case for lack of evidence.

Jay Silver turned the defense of the case over to a litigator, Bradford Hayes, who had a reputation for winning tough cases.

3

Jimmy Stevens, the man who had taken Mulhaney's rifle to the gun range, was hunched over in a chair in the City County Building. Stevens' son had been arrested with a friend after they were caught breaking into a neighbor's house and ransacking the living room. The kids thought the house was empty, but they found out otherwise when the homeowner confronted them with a ball bat. At the time they were holding his t.v. set and a bag of silver-plated flatware. Dumbkidstuff. But the cops were calling it felony robbery with jail time.

"I know you're upset about your boy being arrested, Mr. Stevens," the arresting cop said to Jimmy Stevens.

"It'll kill his mother," Stevens said.

"Maybe it's not that bad. There might be a way around this," the cop said.

"What do you mean?" a distraught Stevens said.

"There's a man from the BATF here. He says maybe you can work something out."

The officer turned toward the quiet man in a suit that was standing nearby. "This is agent Bennington," he said.

Bennington shook hands with Stevens and said, "Mr. Stevens, I don't think this case with your boy needs to go very far, if you can see your way clear to work with us on another thing."

"I'll do anything. What do you want me to do?"

"The Clyde Mulhaney case."

"Yeah Clyde. I just tried to buy a gun."

"Well, maybe you could help us if we asked you a few questions at Mulhaney's trial. Is it possible you and he talked about selling the gun, you know, informally, without bothering to fix it before it got sold? He might even have said he would take less for it if you bought it without getting it fixed. Something like that."

"No he never said anything like that. Neither one of us knew anything was wrong with the gun. In fact, after I brought it back and told him it fired two rounds with one trigger pull, he said he'd have it looked at."

"What if you were to say that he might have said something like that, but you can't remember," the BATF agent said.

"Well, maybe I could do that. What if I said I can't remember because I was so tired that day and upset about the gun not working? If I said that, would that get my boy off?"

"I think that might be enough. I'll have a lawyer from our office talk to you next week. In the meantime, why don't you take your boy on out of here. I'm sure we'll be able to take care of that for you."

"You know, I wouldn't be lying. I would be saying I can't remember him offering to sell the gun for less if I took it broken. And that's true. I can't remember him saying that because he never said it."

"You work it out in your own mind however you want to," Bennington said.

"Oh, Jesus, thank you Mr. Bennington, . . . Agent Bennington. His mother would have a breakdown if she thought he was going to jail. Thanks so much. You won't have any more trouble from him or from me. Thanks again."

* * *

Six months later, the Mulhaney trial was over. Both sides had presented their cases, and the Assistant U.S. Attorney, Donald Thompson, was summing up the government's case.

"Ladies and gentlemen, Clyde Mulhaney comes off-I should say he tries to come off-as the wronged super-patriot. Actually, he's just another low life who is willing to jeopardize your children and mine by selling illegal machine guns.

His own friend told us what happened. Mulhaney tried to sell him an unlicensed machine gun for cash. You can imagine Mulhaney explaining that by paying cash, there would be no record of the transaction, the gun would not be known to the government, and the buyer would simply walk away with an unlicensed machine gun that no one would know he had.

Bradford Hayes, Mulhaney's new lawyer, stood up. "Objection, your honor. The government lawyer is stating facts not in the record. There was no testimony that such a conversation took place."

The court said, "Overruled, Mr. Hayes. You'll have your chance. Sit down."

Hayes sat down, obviously upset.

The government lawyer continued, "Look at who this man is. He has three of these rifles. Admittedly, two of them were not machine guns, but they were the same as the machine gun except that they required the pulling of the trigger for each shot. Now here's my question to you. Who needs three of these guns? And even worse, what are these guns for? They're no good for hunting. The answer is simple. These guns have one purpose and only one purpose: they are for killing people. Mulhaney himself used a gun like these in Iraq. His job? To kill people.

"Objection, your honor," Hayes spat out. "Mulhaney's possession of legally owned semi-automatic rifles is not at issue in this case."

"Overruled, Mr. Hayes. Sit down."

"And then you heard the testimony of Mulhaney's neighbors," the government lawyer continued. "According to the people who live close to him, Mulhaney is a strange bird, a loner, and the lights are often on at his house all hours of the night."

Hayes was on his feet again, "Your Honor, I demand that you stop this character assassination. How late Mr. Mulhaney stays up or whether he gets along with his neighbors are not issues in the case."

"I won't tell you again, Mr. Hayes. Sit down. Your objection is overruled."

"You heard Mr. Hayes, ladies and gentlemen," the government lawyer said, "we should not inquire into what kind of a person Mr. Mulhaney is. . . "

"That's right," Hayes erupted. "It is black letter law that a person cannot be convicted of a crime because the prosecutor thinks he is a bad man."

"Sit down, Mr. Hayes. Mr. Thompson, go on with the government's case."

"Well, ladies and gentlemen of the jury, I'll let you decide. It's just common sense to me that a man who would sneak around in the dead of night might also be the type of guy who would sneak around and sell an illegal machine gun."

"Your honor, Please. There is nothing of record about sneaking around."

"Overruled. Go on counselor."

"This case is simple, ladies and gentlemen. Consider what you have before you. You have an illegal machine gun. Nothing Mr. Hayes says can change that. You have the testimony of Mulhaney's own friend that Mulhaney tried to convince him he should buy an illegal machine gun and that no one would ever know. And you have the testimony of Mulhaney's neighbors, the people who know him best, that Mulhaney is a shady character, the type of man who would put other people in jeopardy just so he could make a buck.

"When you put all this together, really, you have no choice. You must find him guilty as charged."

There was silence in the courtroom as the prosecutor sat down. The judge said, "Mr. Hayes?"

Bradford Hayes stood. He buttoned his coat and approached the jury.

"Ladies and gentlemen, good afternoon. The government attorney has stated the evidence in this case as he apparently remembers it. I don't remember it that way. But it is not important how he remembers it or how I remember it. What is important is how you remember it.

Clyde Mulhaney did nothing wrong. You heard his testimony. He lent a rifle to a friend who expressed an interest in buying it. When the friend took the rifle to the range, it malfunctioned and began to fire automatically. You will recall the testimony of our expert to the effect that rifles such as this can sometimes malfunction when they are worn or when, as here, hundreds of rounds are shot out of them in a short time. The fact that the rifle malfunctioned does not make it an illegal weapon. It is a legal weapon that needed to be repaired.

"The government would have you believe that Mulhaney's purpose was to sell an illegal machine gun. If that is so, why would he send his friend out to a public gun range where the gun would be identified as a machine gun. And if it was a machine gun, why didn't it fire automatically for the first 900 rounds that Mr. Stevens put through it that day?

"And let's go to Mr. Stevens' testimony. The government says that Stevens testified that Mulhaney wanted to sell him a machine gun secretly and for cash. What Stevens actually said was that he couldn't remember whether such a conversation took place.

"Consider that. If someone has offered to sell you an illegal machine gun, you're likely to remember, aren't you? In fact, I imagine it would he hard to get it out of your mind. But Mr. Stevens can't remember. I suggest to you that Mr. Stevens' testimony is unbelievable. If there had been such a conversation, he would have remembered every word.

"So why is his memory suddenly so bad? And by the way, Mr. Mulhaney and his wife tell me that they have lived in their neighborhood for ten years and that they have never had anything but cordial relations with their neighbors. In fact, there are neighborhood picnics and gatherings that they and others participate in regularly. So why are the neighbors suddenly so negative about Mr. Mulhaney?

"Objection," Mr. Thompson said, "summation based on information not in evidence."

"Sustained. The jury will disregard the comment about what was said to counsel out of court. Be careful Mr. Hayes."

"All right, your Honor. Let me ask you this, ladies and gentlemen, if the BATF is capable of breaking down Clyde Mulhaney's door and sticking a gun in his face and terrorizing his family, when they come to your house to ask about Mulhaney, are you going to be likely to tell them what they want to hear?"

"Objection, your Honor. There is no evidence that the BATF coerced anyone," Thompson said.

"Overruled. He is only raising it as a possibility."

"Thank you your Honor. That's right. It is a possible explanation of why neighbors testified as they did. But even if their testimony is true-which it is not-it is irrelevant to the issues in this case. Whether Clyde Mulhaney is a loner or whether he stays up late at night has nothing to do with whether he intentionally tried to sell an illegal machine gun. What is interesting, however, and what you should pay attention to, is why the neighbors would say these things.

"Let's go back to Mr. Stevens. Insofar as the government has a case against Mr. Mulhaney at all, it is through the testimony of Mr. Stevens-a man who can't remember whether Mr. Mulhaney intentionally tried to sell him an illegal machine gun. You will recall that on cross-examination, I asked Mr. Stevens whether he had a son named Shawn, and, over Mr. Thompson's objection, he was directed to answer. You will recall he testified that he does have a son named Shawn, that Shawn was arrested for robbery, and that, without explanation, the charges against Shawn were withdrawn.

"I will leave it to you to decide whether there is any connection between Mr. Stevens' bad memory and his son's fortunate escape from the legal system.

"Mr. Thompson has attempted to paint Mr. Mulhaney as a bad person merely because he owns guns. Who would own such guns, he asks you, especially since they aren't good for hunting. Yet Mr. Thompson knows full well that there is nothing wrong with owning guns of the sort Mr. Mulhaney owned. These guns are not illegal. The only issue in the case is whether Mr. Mulhaney is to be treated as a criminal because one of his legally owned guns malfunctioned.

"When I encounter arguments such as the arguments Mr. Thompson has made in this case, I am ashamed of my profession. Mr. Thompson knows that the United States Supreme Court has held that there is an individual right in the United States to own weapons for self-defense. This right-this Constitutional right-has nothing to do with hunting. And yet Mr. Thompson would have you condemn this man because he owned weapons that the United States Supreme Court says he has a right to own.

"We are in Pennsylvania, and although this is a federal court, federal courts are required to uphold state law when it is not in conflict with federal law. The Pennsylvania Constitution provides: 'The right of citizens to bear arms in defense of themselves and the state shall not be questioned.' This Pennsylvania constitutional provision does not conflict with the Second Amendment to the United States Constitution, and in fact, it may give Pennsylvania citizens even more rights to own firearms than the federal constitution.

"In sum, Clyde Mulhaney is not a bad man because he owns weapons the constitutions of our country and our state says he may own, whether or not they are for hunting. Beyond that, as I said earlier, the state's entire case is based on the testimony-the unbelievable testimony-of Mr. Stevens. If you disbelieve Stevens-and there is no reason to believe him-you must find the my client not guilty."

The jury deliberated three hours. At the end of that time, they found Mulhaney guilty on both counts charged--unlawful possession of an unlicensed machine gun and unlawful attempt to transfer an unlicensed machine gun. Sentencing was to take place in thirty days.

Three days after the conviction, Mulhaney lost his job.

4

A few weeks after the Mulhaney trial, Sam Budda sat at a table in an interrogation room in the federal building in downtown Pittsburgh. A muscular young man, BATF agent Dennis Ivory, glared at Budda and paced around the room. Concrete block walls were painted with light green semi gloss paint. There were no pictures. The standard two-way mirror was mounted in the middle of the wall opposite the door.

"I'm gonna give you one more chance to tell me who this guy is-this client of yours," Agent Ivory said.

"I've told you all I know. I was hired by a client whose identity I do not know, to deliver a message to you. The message is that if your agency does not back off of the Mulhaney case, the client will start shooting ATF agents. I showed you the postal money order he sent to pay my fee and his letter requesting my services. That's all I know and that's all I have to say."

"Sure, that has to be right, Budda. People just call you up and tell you to go threaten to murder federal agents and you don't know nothing about it."

"What I know is what I've told you."

A third man, also an ATF agent, stood in the corner, chewing a toothpick watching Sam. The third man carried a pistol in a cross-draw belt holster and slouched against the wall with his arms folded. Ivory mumbled "piece a shit" under his breath. Sam stared straight ahead.

Periodically Agent Ivory would ask a question that implicated Sam in the threats made by his clients, and Sam would remain silent. Then the young agent would say something to the man in the corner, who would snicker.

The door opened and an older agent motioned to Ivory to come out. The older agent, Randy Jenkins, said, "Dennis, we can't find out who this guy is."

"What the hell does that mean?" Ivory said.

"Our computer search gives date of birth, driver's license, p.i. license, address, stuff like that, but it blocks any in-depth stuff. And the code blocking it is the Pentagon," Jenkins said.

"Why would the Pentagon block this jerk's information?"

"He probably was a private contractor for some hi-end agency at one time. As far as we can tell, he doesn't work for any federal agency right now."

"Fuck this guy," Ivory said. "He thinks he can come in here with his bullshit about unknown clients and his private eye license and threaten us. He thinks he's tough."

Jenkins led Ivory into the viewing area behind the one-way glass of the interrogation room.

"Go easy, Dennis," he said. "Look at this guy."

Jenkins pointed to the man in the chair.

"Look at the way he sits in that chair. He's in no hurry. He's not afraid. He's not concerned about anything you've said to him. You're not gonna rattle him. I'd be careful if I were you. You don't know who he is," Jenkins said.

"So what?"

"You listen to me Dennis. I been around here a lot longer than you have. You still think that you're invulnerable because you got a badge. I'm telling you, it don't work that way, and right now is a good time to keep that in mind. This guy could hurt you. You don't know. Be careful."

Ivory walked back into the interrogation room. Sam didn't move or show any interest in the agent's re-entry. The young man leaned on the table with his face inches from Sam's nose, "Let's go over this again. What makes you think you can come in here and tell us you're gonna shoot ATF agents?"

Without moving, Sam said, "I've said all I have to say."

"Yeah? Well, I'm not through with you. You'll stay here as long as I say."

" I've already been here four hours. You have to arraign me or let me go in another two."

"Really? You know the law. Now you're a jailhouse lawyer."

The agent slouching in the corner snickered.

Ivory walked around the table, approaching Sam from the side. He got down close to Sam's ear and said quietly, "What if some of my friends and I run into you one night?"

"I'd deal with it."

"Oh. Really? How would you deal with it?"

Sam said nothing.

"Come on, tough guy. What would you do?"

Sam looked at the young agent and said, "Guys like you run in packs and you're tough when your friends are all there or when your victim is in handcuffs."

"Is that a threat? We'll see who gets hurt."

Sam remained silent and looked straight ahead.

"The computer says you're Sam Budda, some kind of hard-ass spook."

"Really? But that doesn't concern you does it?"

"No, it doesn't concern me. You know why? Cause I know what you are. You're a bottom feeder."

Sam said nothing.

"Nothing to say?"

Sam said, "A lot of years ago I was in a room like this and there was a prick behaving just like you."

"Yeah? Spook stuff, huh?"

"He was hitting on this other guy, and the other guy just sat there. The prick hit him with a hose. He then he started yelling at him and he put his face up real close, just like you did. The guy grabbed the prick, pulled him over the table and broke his neck. He took the prick's gun and let himself out of the room."

"Wow. Quite a story. So is that what you're gonna do, tough guy? Break my neck? Here, let me get up real close so you can grab me."

Ivory stuck his face in Sam's. The agent in the corner, pushed off the wall and moved forward in case Budda tried to pull him over the table.

"Just a story," Sam whispered without taking his eyes off the ATF man. His nose was almost touching the young agent's nose. "Just a story, Agent Dennis Ivory," he said.

Ivory held his face inches from Budda's face for a minute longer, staring into Sam's eyes. Budda didn't flinch.

"You remember, Budda, I may come visit you some night when there are no witnesses, and if I do, you will get hurt. Some dark night, tough guy. Sometime when you aren't expecting it."

"Are you though with me?" Sam asked.

"Oh no. You go to the lockup and we go to your house."

* * *

A pair of black Ford Crown Victorias pulled up in front of Sam Budda's house in Bloomfield. Two ATF agents got out of each car, and approached the front door. They all wore blue nylon windbreakers with large yellow BATF letters on the back. One bulky agent struggled with a large canvas bag containing the hydraulic jack that ATF favored for removing doors from door jams. The agents mounted the front steps and the last dropped the canvas bag on the porch with a metallic clank. As he was unzipping the bag, Nick Savarese, Sam Budda's partner, opened the door. Beside him, Ronin, a 150 pound Akita, stood silently, glaring at the agent who was unpacking the jack.

"Who the hell are you?" the fat agent said, out of breath from walking up the steps.

"I'm Mr. Budda's business partner. He told me you might be coming and asked me to open the house for you."

"Is that dog under control?" another agent said.

Ronin stood in a stiff-legged stance next to Nick, clearly on alert.

"He's fine," Nick said. "He won't bother you."

"You just keep him away from me. That sonofabitch doesn't look under control to me."

"I told you, he won't bother you.

"If he does, we'll shoot him. Just so you know," another agent said.

"You come to my house and threaten to shoot my dog. I'd think that through if I were you," Nick said.

"You're under arrest," the agent snarled. "You're threatening a federal officer."

"You're under arrest," the agent snarled. "You're threatening a federal officer."

Ronin began a low growl and stared at the agent with the blank look that a Komodo dragon has when he is contemplating his next meal. Before the agent could arrest Nick, the front door opened further and an elderly man in a gray suit stepped out.

"I'm Bradford Hayes," he said. "I am an attorney and I represent Mr. Budda and Mr. Savarese. We are not here to stand in your way, agent, or to cause trouble. Mr. Savarese is here to let you into the house and to open whatever secure area you need to inspect."

"I don't give a fuck who you are," the agent said, now openly belligerent, "He's under arrest for threatening a federal agent. You get in my way, I'll arrest you too."

Bradford Hayes was nothing if not a gentleman, and it was not his style to respond in kind. He was accustomed to dealing with police.

"Mr. Savarese did not threaten you. As a matter of fact, you threatened him. If you arrest him, or me, I will file a civil suit against you and your agency this afternoon for violation of our civil rights—it's called deprivation of constitutional rights under color of law—and I will file complaints directly with the Justice Department in Washington. I've done this before. You'll end up unemployed."

Hayes' voice was even. His demeanor calm, not threatening. He was a surgeon waiting to see if he had to cut them open or not.

The ATF agents looked at each other. Ronin continued his barely audible growl, his lower lip quivering slightly.

"Now I suggest," Hayes said, "that you fellows just get on with your work. I understand that you want to install some telephone listening equipment. And if you have a search warrant of some kind, you're free to look around to the extent that the warrant allows it. Do you have a warrant?"

One of the agents handed Hayes a folded paper.

"This gives you authority to install a listening and tracing device on Mr. Budda's phone line," he said. "Nothing more."

"All right, counselor, you and the dog-man here just stay out of our way."

For the next hour, the agents attached electronic devices to Sam's phone line, taking every opportunity to bump into furniture, scuff their shoes on the hardwood floors, knock over lamps, and leave trash wherever they went.

At 1:12 p.m., the phone rang. An ATF agent answered.

"Yeah."

The voice on the line was electronically scrambled. "Let me speak to Sam Budda."

"This is Sam Budda," the agent said.

"No, you are probably with the ATF," the voice said. "We knew you would be there. Put Sam Budda on."

"Who is we?" the agent said.

"I'll call again in an hour. You put Budda on or get out the body bags," the voice said.

Numbers flashed on one of the tracing machines. The agent on the phone looked hopefully at the tracing operators.

"Nothing," the operator said. "He's got this call switching from one number to another. When he hung up, he was calling from Morocco. Before that, it was Hong Kong."

The agent with the phone said, "You heard him. He wants Budda. If Budda will keep him on the line, maybe we can get a location."

"Okay," the senior agent said. "Get Budda out of the lockup. Bring him here."

* * *

When Sam walked into his living room, Ronin met him with an Akita greeting—growling,—shaking his head and grabbing Sam's wrist in his mouth. Ronin's whole body moved as he wagged his tail. Sam petted his dog and knelt down and hugged him. He surveyed the equipment all over his living room and the debris, wire shavings, and candy wrappers that littered the room. The phone rang just as the senior agent was telling Sam what to say.

"Hello," Sam answered.

"Hello, Budda," the electronic voice said. "I see they brought you back."

Recorders were in motion and the digital tracing machine was flashing through one digital sequence after another.

"Yeah, they brought me back," Sam said.

"Did they lock you up after you gave them our first message?"

"Yes."

"We have another message."

"Why not talk to them directly?" Sam said. "They're all around here. They can just walk over to the phone."

"No, Budda. We talk to you, not them."

"Why? I don't know you. I can't help you."

"We want you, Budda, because we want someone to know everything we're doing. If we talk to them, they'll twist what we say and they'll cover it up. If you're involved and they want to cover it up, they'll have to kill you or buy you off. We want a record."

"Thanks for putting me in the crosshairs," Sam said.

"Here's the message. If the BATF does not stop the Mulhaney prosecution we'll start killing their agents. That's the message."

"I already gave them that message."

"We're repeating it because they didn't listen. Instead, they threw you in jail and tapped your phones. This is their last chance to save some lives."

The call ended. Sam stood with the receiver in his hand, looking at the agents. This time the call originated in the Ukraine.

* * *

That evening, the light of a big screen television flickered through the curtains of the Jancey Street residence of Agent Dennis Ivory. The doorbell rang and Sara Ivory, a petite blonde in her early thirties, answered the door, wiping her hands on a dish towel.

The man at the door, wearing a black fedora and dressed in a suit and tie partially covered by an overcoat, said, "Mrs. Ivory?"

"Yes."

He raised his right hand and shot her twice in the chest with a silenced Walther. The only sound was the metallic cycling of the slide. As her knees collapsed, the assailant grabbed her around the waist and dragged her into the foyer before closing the door.

The light thump of the woman's body falling to the floor was vaguely audible in the living room. "Sara?" Ivory called from the living room. "Who's there?"

Silence.

Dennis Ivory rose from the couch and walked barefoot to the arch separating the living room from the foyer. He froze when he saw his wife's body, a slight pool of blood collecting under her elbow.

The first of two bullets hit Ivory in the face as he glanced toward a figure standing in the corner. He was dead when police arrived hours later in response to calls from the neighbors that the front door was standing open.

5

In the aftermath of the murders of BATF agent Ivory and his wife, Sam Budda was high on the list of suspects, but there was no evidence connecting him to the crime. A week passed with no break in the case. As the shock of the Ivory killing was wearing off, BATF got a call from Budda that his client had another message. The client was going to send a letter to the Pittsburgh Post Gazette concerning the Mulhaney case. If BATF interfered with the publication of this letter, the client said, he would start killing BATF agents. Budda spoke with Corky James, the head of the BATF office in Pittsburgh. James asked Budda to come in to the BATF office.

Sam arrived in James' office on the sixth floor of the federal building later that morning. Sam was shown into James' office and was told to sit in a wooden office chair with arms, right out of the 30's, facing James, who sat behind an oversized mahogany desk designed to make him look important. Without any preliminaries, James said, "Look, Budda, your 'client'-James held up to fingers to put quotes around 'client'-is in a shitload of trouble, and unless you help us on this, so are you,"

"I am helping you," Budda said.

"How are you helping?"

"He calls me and I forward the message to you."

"That's not what I mean, and you know it."

"That's all I can do. You seem to think I know who this guy is, but I don't. I've told you that."

"Have you seen the letter he wants published in the Post Gazette?"

"No."

"Let me read it to you.

You all know about the Mulhaney case. An innocent man is about to go to jail. Some of us won't let that happen. Everybody who reads this should use whatever influence they have to get this stopped. If that influence isn't enough, we will start killing BATF agents until they let Mulhaney go. We don't want to kill agents, but we will if that's what it takes.

The Patriots

"Did the Patriot send it to you?" Sam said.

"No. He sent it to the Post Gazette, and the newspaper faxed it to us. They want to know whether they should publish it," James said.

"What did you tell them?" Sam asked.

"I told them hell no. I told them this guy is just looking for publicity and they'd be playing into his hands."

"I don't get that impression from talking to him," Sam said. "I think he's serious. I think you should be careful with this guy. Not blow him off."

"I know you're a big shot, at least in your own mind, but you don't tell me how to do my job. Got it?"

"I'm just using common sense, James. Don't piss this guy off."

"Get out of my office, Budda. If we had the slightest thing on you, I'd lock you up. This is the federal government you're messing with, and finally you'll come to grief-you and your secret friend. We'll find him, and when we do, I'll bet we'll find that you're involved."

"Take care, Agent James," Sam said, walking out the door.

Meanwhile, across town the editors of the Post Gazette were meeting.

"Just read it, Joshua," the city editor said.

"All right," Higgins said. "The cover letter says, 'If you do not publish this notice in tomorrow's paper, we will start killing ATF agents. If you do publish it, we will hold off a few days to give them time to let Mulhaney go.'

"Here's what they want us to publish."

You all know about the Mulhaney case. An innocent man is about to go to jail. Some of us won't let that happen. Everybody who reads this should use whatever influence they have to get this stopped. If that influence isn't enough, we will start killing BATF agents until they let Mulhaney go. We don't want to kill agents, but we will if that's what it takes.

The Patriots

"I think it's a crock," the sports editor snorted.

"'The Patriots,' my ass. Joshua, we get this stuff all the time. What grabs you about this one?" the city editor said.

"I know, I know," Higgins said. "It's probably nothing,"

"Joshua," an old man in the back said. "Trust your instincts. You brought this in here. You didn't think it was fluff."

The old man was City Editor Emeritus Edge Dixon, who was invited periodically to sit in on editorial meetings, where his insights, balance and wisdom were usually well-received.

"My gut tells me this guy is serious," Higgins said. "This whole thing reminds me of what happened at Ruby Ridge and Waco, Texas."

"You sound like the gun nut who wrote that silly thing you're holding," the Sports Editor said.

"I don't own a gun, Jim," Higgins said.

"I said you sound like him, not that you own a gun."

"Nobody hates the whole gun bullshit more than I do, Jim. You know that. But when the police start beating down doors of some guy like Mulhaney, they play into the hands of the gun nuts. The last time that happened, we got Oklahoma City."

The city editor said, "But BATF, and the FBI, for that matter, have already been discredited, Joshua. There were senate hearings and the FBI sniper, Horiuchi, or something, the one that killed Randy Weaver's wife-he was prosecuted. They wouldn't be going out on the same limb three times.

Dixon, the Editor Emeritus, said, "You're wrong about the prosecution. The state district attorney brought involuntary manslaughter charges against Horiuchi in state court, but Horiuchi was successful in removing the case to federal court. The federal trial court held that he could not be prosecuted for acts he committed as a federal agent, but the federal appeals court reversed and sent the case back to state court for trial. By then, however, a new district attorney had been elected, and he refused to bring the case to trial. Horiuchi was never tried for his crime."

"Okay," the City Editor said, "but they charged him. And in any case, ATF is pretty much the laughing stock of law enforcement. You remember from those hearings how they activated an AWACS plane to fly overhead and sent armored personnel carriers and an army to go after one guy living in a plywood shack with his wife and kids? Who would take them seriously after that?"

Higgins put the letter down, shaking his head, when the old man spoke up. "Clyde Mulhaney."

"What?" the editor said.

"Clyde Mulhaney. He would take them seriously after that. He's rousted out of his bed by men in black suits who break his jaw, give him a concussion, and put rifles to his head. His wife is beaten senseless and hospitalized and his kids are terrorized. He would take the BATF very seriously after that."

"Look," the City Editor said, "We don't really know what happened with Mulhaney, but if you two are so worried about this, why don't you send this whole thing over to ATF. Let them figure out what they want to do."

"They already have it. I faxed it over to them."

"What do they want us to do?"

"James, the head guy at BATF, wants us to suppress it."

"Then what's the problem? They want it suppressed? We kill it."

"It's not that easy. I don't think they're going to warn their people that a threat is out there. They don't want to any controversy about what they do and how they do it."

"Fine. If they don't want to us to publish it, why do we want to publish it? Shouldn't that be ATF's call?" the sports editor said. "If they don't warn their people, that's on them."

"Besides, if they want it suppressed, maybe they're right," the City Editor said. Maybe we would just be encouraging these nuts by publishing the letter."

"And maybe they're not right," the Editor Emeritus said. "They're bureaucrats, for Christ's sake. What do you expect them to say? They don't want any negative publicity about what they've done. Maybe by not publishing the letter, the first indication this threat exists will be the corpse of another ATF agent."

* * *

Agent John Kaplan had been with the ATF five years. He joined right out of college because he was attracted to the promise of adventure and the prestige of carrying a federal badge. He was 28 years old. The job was not as exciting as he had been led to believe, but that was bothered him less that the redneck attitude of the other agents in his office. There was an ex-city cop, a few army non-coms, and a lot of bureaucrats from federal and state government. None of them seemed to have any inclination to think for themselves.

Fresh out of college, Kaplan believed in the rule of law and fair play. After a few months in the agency, however, he learned that those ideas were not very useful if you wanted to go somewhere in the agency. And Kaplan did. It wasn't like the city police, where overt bribes were the norm. Instead, at ATF it was more like there was a company agenda which, if you bought into it, you succeeded. If you didn't, your career withered. It was hard to describe the agenda, but it had to do with pumping the agency up, being one of the agency boys, always assuming the suspect was guilty, looking down on local and other federal law enforcement, and above all, taking every opportunity to get guns out of the hands of citizens.

It wasn't a matter of taking bribes, at least at the level Kaplan had experienced. It was more about acquiring and exercising power. The more power the better.

Like all youngsters coming into new jobs, Kaplan was at a disadvantage. He had no other work experience and no real background in ethics or law. The practices and culture of the agency seemed to go against what he had learned in school, but the guys who ran the agency were highly placed federal officials, so why worry about it?

He went along and was rewarded with promotions, salary increases and assignment to the "Combat Team," as the black suited response team of Pittsburgh ATF was called. Along with twenty or thirty others, Kaplan got to dress up in black combat fatigues, put on a black helmet and face shield, and carry a black rifle.

After his usual Thursday night basketball game at one of the courts at the University of Pittsburgh, Kaplan walked the block from the gym to a university parking garage. He entered the garage, paid for his ticket at the machine on the first floor, and took the stairs to the third floor, where his car was parked.

Kaplan walked up the the stairwell to the level where he was parked and dug in his left front pocket for his keys. As he was entered the level where his car was parked, he noticed a shape on the garage floor twenty yards ahead. It was a man slumped over moaning and holding his stomach.

"Jesus Christ," Kaplan murmured to himself. He jogged toward the old man, dropped his gym bag, and knelt down. "Are you all right?"

The man, who had been curled up in a fetal position facing away from Kaplan, rolled over, grabbed Kaplan's collar, pulled him off balance and downward until their faces almost touched. The man jammed a Colt .45 into Kaplan's chest and fired two quick rounds on contact. Kaplan was dead before his body hit the cement. The round that ripped through Kaplan's heart was a Federal Hydra-Shock. Both rounds mushroomed to .78 caliber as they were designed to do, and they penetrated Kaplan's back, leaving gaping exit wounds.

The old man used his grip on Kaplan's collar to roll the falling body away from him. He engaged the Colt's safety, surveyed the garage for witnesses, and placed a photocopy of the letter sent to the Post Gazette on Kaplan's chest, stuck between the buttons of his shirt.

* * *

The story in the Pittsburgh Post Gazette read:

> *The body of John Kaplan, an agent of the Bureau of Alcohol, Tobacco and Firearms, was discovered yesterday in a parking garage near the field house at the University of Pittsburgh. He was shot to death with a handgun at very close range. Police have found no witnesses to the shooting. Kaplan had been playing basketball in an intramural league and was found near his car.*
>
> *Pittsburgh Police reported that a photocopy of a letter that had been sent to this newspaper was found on Kaplan's body. The letter read:*
>
> *If you do not publish this letter in tomorrow's paper, we will start killing ATF agents. If you do publish it, we will give ATF time to let Mulhaney go.*
>
> *Here's what the letter asked the PG to publish:*
>
> *You all know about the Mulhaney case. An innocent man is about to go to jail. Some of us won't let that happen. Everybody who reads this should use whatever influence they have to get this stopped. If that influence isn't enough, we will start killing BATF agents until they let Mulhaney go. We don't want to kill agents, but we will if that's what it takes*
>
> *The Patriots*
>
> *The Post Gazette very much regrets the death of Agent Kaplan. We did not publish this letter at the request of the BATF.*

6

Six weeks before Agent Kaplan was killed in the parking garage on the Pitt campus, three old men sat at their table in a restaurant on Pittsburgh's south side reading the Post Gazette. The Mulhaney story, which regularly appeared in the papers since the initial BATF invasion of the Mulhaney home, now concerned the end of the trial. The newspaper reported Mulhaney's conviction of the felony of possessing and attempting to sell a machine gun. Various legal experts were quoted as saying that the case was most unusual and that the verdict would surely be appealed. The story also reported that Mulhaney had lost his job. Mulhaney continued to maintain his innocence, saying that the gun had simply malfunctioned. Mulhaney's lawyer, Bradford Hayes, promised an appeal was forthcoming and that justice would be done.

The old men, one an American Indian, one black, one an American Jew, were regular customers at Sadie's Restaurant. They had met for breakfast every day for the last ten years, and they had known each other for many years before that.

The conversation between the old men, which seemed to ebb and flow for some time, was intense. They were concentrated on the newspaper and occasionally one of them would read a passage aloud.

The three had been friends since the Second World War, when they served in the same unit. They had gone ashore together on the same LST on D Day and had fought through North Africa and Sicily before that. For nearly sixty years, they had looked after each other, and they thought of each other as brothers.

Jamie Berenger was a Navajo Code Talker from the Four Corners area who, during the war, insisted on carrying a rifle; Aaron Silverman was a Jew from Pittsburgh's south side; Jesse Washington was a black man who had grown up in Pittsburgh's Homestead section. They were all withered to some degree, all a little hunched, but each did some form of military workout every day and each was in good health. Aaron and Jamie Berenger had thick white hair; Jesse was bald. All three wore baseball caps with a military flair, two fingers above the eyebrows.

A pitcher of coffee sat in the middle of the table, and first one, then another, reached over to pour another cup.

"Mulhaney's lawyer says justice will be done," Jamie Berenger said.

Jesse guffawed.

"The check's in the mail," Aaron said.

"They're gonna fry the sonofabitch," Jesse said. "It's as good as done."

"Unless somebody saves him," Jamie said.

"Who's gonna do that?" Jesse said. "The government's got everybody scared silly. You go against the government, you end up like Mulhaney."

"It's the same tactics as Hitler," Aaron said.

Jamie said, "Whenever the government's got everybody scared shitless, nobody will stand up for what's right. At that point, you're in a goddam dictatorship. It looks like that's what's happening here. We may as well be back in Nazi Germany."

Jamie Berenger was in a reflective mood. His face was handsomely lined, full of arroyos, and the color of the New Mexico desert. He rolled up the long sleeves of his heavy flannel shirt as he talked.

"We were all there at Dachau. We all walked through that camp and felt those skeleton fingers touch our GI jackets, those fingers that looked like twigs, and we saw them look at us with those hollow dead eyes. We said we never wanted to see anything like that again. It was something that stuck with us. We can't forget it, and we've said we'd never let that happen here. Remember when we learned about the Warsaw Ghetto? How a few guys with a few weapons held off the whole German army. If those skeletons in the camps had a few weapons, they could have too."

"Hitler took their weapons. Now our own government is taking ours," Jamie Berenger said.

He took a long drink of black coffee and looked at his comrades.

Jamie Berenger had grown up on a reservation not far from Albuquerque. Like all the men in his family, he had been raised a hunter and a rifleman. He had grown up around guns and around the outdoors. His first real exposure to white men was in the war, when he and other Navajos were recruited as Code Talkers. He spent six months as a code talker, and then insisted on going into the infantry. He didn't feel comfortable without a rifle.

When Jamie Berenger was transferred to the regular infantry, he kept to himself, though he distinguished himself on the rifle range. Aaron Silverman and Jesse Washington, who were expert marksmen themselves, saw how well he could shoot, and they sought him out. The three became fast friends. They were constant companions and they were experts with the M1 Garand. After the war, they went their separate ways, but promised to stay in touch. Jamie Berenger, wanting to stay near his friends who were in Pennsylvania, moved to central Ohio and went to work in a local gun shop. He had been trained as an armourer in the army, and he had instruction from his father before that in fixing weapons. After a year working for the gun shop, he went off on his own and opened a small gun repair shop in Bowling Green, Ohio. His business was doing well when a neighboring shopkeeper, who didn't like Indians or guns called the police and reported that Jamie was a fence for stolen firearms. The police came to his shop and seized every gun in the shop, regardless of whom it belonged to. Eight months later, they released all of the guns, but by then, Jamie's business was ruined and on the verge of bankruptcy.

Jamie Berenger was angry that the government had simply put him out of business and then denied any responsibility. His friend Aaron got him a job on a construction project in Pittsburgh, and he spent the next thirty years working on construction in Pennsylvania.

Aaron said, "You're right. We said we'd never let it happen here. But it has. They busted into this guy's house, terrorized his family, stole his property, and prosecuted him on charges that will end up putting him in prison. Throw in concentration camps, and it sounds pretty much like Hitler."

Aaron Silverman was fragile-looking, but those who knew him never thought of him as frail. A recurring nightmare for Aaron was that he was a small boy hidden in the woods, watching as his neighbors and his relatives were marched to the the edge of a pit, shot and killed, and toppled over into the pit, which served as a mass grave. He had other dreams too where his relatives and neighbors were lined up at railroad stations and shipped to places like Dachau, where they gassed them. Sometimes his dreams fastened on his relatives being herded onto platforms and pushed into suffocating stock cars with no food, no sanitary facilities, no heat, no room to even sit down. In some of the dreams, his parents died in the cattle cars standing up.

Aaron almost never slept soundly, and when he did, he would awake, having imagined himself suffocating at the bottom of a cattle car. He was being crushed, unable to stand or even breathe. No Jew had a gun. They had no means to resist. The cattle car was a tomb.

Aaron grew up in Pittsburgh's south side. His father was a doctor. Dr. Silverman's office was four blocks from his house on Carson Street, and he would care for anyone who walked in, whether they could pay or not. As a result, Aaron's father never earned much money, but he instilled in his sons that service to the collective community, not getting rich, was the measure of success in life.

Dr. Silverman lost his mother and father and two brothers in the Warsaw Ghetto.

After the war ended and Aaron returned to life in Pittsburgh, working as a counselor in a center for troubled youth, his father ran into difficulty with the Immigration and Naturalization Service. It was the middle of the 1950's and anti-communism was the political correctness of the day. Because Aaron's father treated some homeless people who could not pay and who were thought to have communist leanings, the father was accused of being a Red sympathizer and threatened with deportation. It seems that the doctor, a Polish national, had never gone though the process to become a citizen.

As visits from the federal bureaucrats became more frequent, Aaron could see that his father was becoming more and more agitated. As the INS inquiries into his presence in the country continued, Dr. Silverman became increasingly enfeebled and took to his bed. In the end, he had a heart attack and died. Aaron buried his father, bitter that his service to his country and his father's dedication to his community meant nothing.

Jesse spoke up. "We talked about it many times over the years, because there were signs. . . . we all seen the signs that the government wasn't right. But none of us wanted to believe what we saw. We told each other it was just the times, just a mistake, just a strangeness that wouldn't come back.

"Then it came back. They busted into Mulhaney's house just like it was the normal thing to do. But it ain't normal, brothers, and it's time for us old guys to stop talkin' and start doin' what we always said we'd do."

Jesse looked more like a middle-aged body builder than an eighty-year-old. His biceps bulged his sleeves and his chest stretched the cotton shirt tight. Strong lines ran down his neck to powerful shoulders. He worked out daily with dumb bells and he walked nearly everywhere. His gaze was steady and his face a deep ebony.

Jesse grew up in Homestead, Pennsylvania, a steel mill town a few miles down the Monongahela River from Pittsburgh. It was a childhood where the schools were substandard, the kids were rough, the neighborhood was rougher, and the mills belched black smoke and soot that blanketed the entire town.

At the end of the war, Jesse and one of his brothers opened a service station on the outskirts of town. The police, mostly the local white boys Jesse had grown up with, made it clear they didn't care for niggers running a service station, and the cops would routinely find some pretext to stop a car that turned in for gas.

Jesse never complained about their interference with his business. He accepted it as a part of life, albeit an unwelcome one, and he concentrated on building the business. Gradually business improved and the brothers always had money to deposit in the bank. Because Jesse was the better mechanic of the two, and found himself covered with grease at quitting time, Jesse's brother usually took the money to the bank. Every day, about 6:30 p.m., he would take the proceeds for the day into town and put it in the night depository at the Mellon Bank. Homestead was still a fairly rough town, and the brother carried a pistol in his belt when he transported the money. In their third year of operation, the local police stopped the brother on his way to the bank. No one was sure what happened. The police would later claim they pulled him over for a traffic violation, and he got out of the car with a gun in his hand. The two policemen fired twelve rounds at him, hitting him four times. When the medical examiner arrived, the brother's handgun was still in his belt, though the police claimed they shot because he was pointing a gun at them.

Jesse had never been a fan of the police, but after his brother's death, he hated and feared them. He no longer had a taste for the service station business, and he spent the next thirty years driving a dump truck.

"Yeah, it's time we did something. The government in Germany came in with force and turned those people's lives upside down. That's just what happened to this guy Mulhaney,"

Aaron said. "Hell, it's what they did to my own father."

"We're old guys now," Jamie Berenger said. "We're not dead. We're just old. And we got nothing to lose. So let's take these bastards on."

"They been doing this stuff for some time," Jesse said. "And we just watched 'em do it."

"We thought they had finally changed," Aaron said. "You remember a few years ago when the FBI sniper killed that guy's wife out in Idaho, and then they killed all those people at Waco. There were hearings and investigations, and we thought they had been exposed and they wouldn't act like that anymore."

"But they're back at it," Jamie Berenger said. "We can't let this one slide. I didn't risk my life all through Europe so I could come home and see the government doing here what the Nazis did there."

"I remember those landings we did like they were yesterday. All those young men-just like us--floating face down in the water. They were just kids. We were just kids, all dressed up in battle gear. Rifles, helmets, harnesses, ammunition, canteens.

But that gear didn't help none did it? Remember when we came off of them boats and started wading through that water, and it had already turned red? And then when we got on the beachhead, death all around us, scared shitless, ordinance going off everywhere, sand blowing in our faces, and us hugging our rifles to our chests as we crawled over those legs and hands and pieces of bodies you couldn't even identify?

"Well, I didn't go through all that so we could come home and watch the government take away the same freedoms too many of us died for."

"You're right," Aaron said. "What do you think we ought to do?"

"Let's think on it and talk again tomorrow," Jesse said.

7

The next morning found the three old men at their table in the South Side restaurant. Coffee steamed in their mugs and the waitress exchanged their exhausted stainless carafe for a fresh one.

"I must be getting old," Jamie said. "I couldn't sleep at all last night. I must'a turned over a thousand times. How about you guys."

"Same here," Aaron said.

"Me too," Jesse said. "I think what bothers me the most is that we're going against our own government."

Jamie said, "First of all Jesse, this government-the one that invaded that guy's house and stuck guns up people's noses-that isn't my government. And secondly, us old guys are probably the only ones who are gonna notice what is going on and take time to resist it. Everybody else is too busy with their jobs and just struggling to stay alive."

"Jamie's right," Aaron said. "Look at us. We're fit enough to stalk an enemy and pull a trigger. If we don't do it, nobody will, and the whole country will be screwed. By the time people know what hit them, it will be too late. They'll be living in a police state."

"Okay," Jesse said, "you're right. Let's do it, but we gotta talk about how we're going to do it."

"Let's get clear about what we are gonna do and what we aren't gonna do," Aaron said. "We're going to be guerilla fighters. We can't win in a straight-up confrontation with the United States government. We have to hit and disappear. We're like the resistance in the War."

"I didn't see no eighty year old resistance fighters," Jesse said.

"I'm tired of hearing about your age, Jesse," Jamie said. "If you're too old for this, bow out."

"No, you're right. I'm just being negative. Forget what I said. I'm in," Jesse said.

"How about this," Aaron said. "We tell BATF what we want and we give them a chance to do it. If they refuse, we start shooting them just like the Jews picked off the Germans in the Warsaw Ghetto, one at a time, when they don't expect it."

"I think we can handle that," Jesse said. "We all can still handle a rifle."

"Don't forget," Jamie said. "We also have the internet. I have the feeling there are a lot of people out there just like us who hate this BATF stuff, but they don't have any way to get themselves organized. We can use the internet to do that."

"Great idea," Aaron said. "As a last resort, we can also use that list. You still got all those names?"

"Hell yeah," Jamie said. "I hacked into that BATF system fifteen years ago and I been keeping up ever since. I got every name and address of BATF agents all over the country. If the goin' gets rough, we publish the names.

"But I been thinkin' about the internet. I suggest we keep our internet exposure down. First of all, I might screw up in hiding our address and do something that would let them find us. Secondly, I think it would be good for us to be able to negotiate with BATF out of the public eye," Jamie said.

"I agree with that,"Jesse said. "They might be more willing to negotiate if the whole world isn't watching them back down."

"Okay," Aaron said. "I've got an idea. You remember a few years back, there was a guy, Jason Hammerlei I think his name was, and this guy was accused of rape. Hammerlei was connected, his family had money because they owned a small steel mill, and he hired Taylor, Sturnbridge, the law firm that used to be downtown."

"Oh yeah," Jesse said. "Didn't they have a big fire?"

"That's the one," Aaron said. "Well my niece Hanna was working in the rape crisis center when this happened, and she was assigned to the rape victim. . . . can't remember her name. My niece would sometimes call the woman on the phone to see how she was, and the woman told her that Hanna didn't need to worry about her any more because she moved in with a roommate and the roommate's brother hired this guy, Sam Budda, to protect both of them."

"Yeah," Jamie said, "I remember the case, but what's it got to do with us."

"This guy, this Budda," Aaron said, "he took on the Hammerlei family and that big law firm and there was some rumor that he was involved in starting the fire in their offices in the Union Trust Building."

"Yeah, I remember now, Jesse said. "But what's that got to do with us?"

"We hire him. We hire Budda," Aaron said.

"Why him?" Jamie said.

"Because he's not afraid to go up against the big money and the big law firms, and because he may not be too concerned about operating outside the law," Aaron said.

Jamie said. "Whatever happened to that rapist, the Hammerlei guy?"

"Rumor has it that Budda and his partner turned Hammerlei over to a motorcycle gang and paid them to rape him. He's in an institution now," Aaron said. "At least that's what my niece told me."

"How would we use this guy?" Jamie said.

"As a go-between," Jamie said. "We talk to him and tell him what to say to BATF."

"What does this get us?" Jesse said.

"For one thing," Aaron said, "we've got somebody out there who knows what is actually happening. If we all die, presumably Budda and his organization will still be alive and able to tell the world."

"You mean you think BATF would cover it up?" Jamie snorted, almost blowing coffee out his nostrils in a fit of mirth.

"This also gives us is a little distance," Jesse said. "I like that. Besides that, this guy Budda sounds fairly tough. That won't do us any harm. If BATF starts pushing him around, he may push back."

"We may also want to use him to get us certain information," Aaron said. "Or we may need him to help with internet stuff, or whatever."

"This sounds good," Jesse said. "What's our next step?"

"Let's send him some money and our message to the BATF," Jamie said. "Let's tell those fuckers to back off Mulhaney or we'll start killing ATF agents. Just that simple."

"Will we actually do it?" Jesse said.

"Hell yes," Aaron said. "Jamie will plan the attacks. We're all good rifle shots. We'll kill them from a distance just like we did in the War. But we won't do nothin' until we give them a chance to back off of Mulhaney."

"It's funny," Jamie Berenger said. "I used to be a hunter. My father raised me to kill game. I did it for many years. Then one year I didn't do it anymore. I didn't want to kill game. I wanted them to live. And now here we are, getting ready to kill people."

8

The Attorney General of the United States, Thomas Carnegie, sat in his office on the sixth floor of the Justice Department at the head of a conference table. His deputy, Ainsworth Bunker-Jones, sat on his right. Sheila Adams, the United States Attorney for the Western District of Pennsylvania (Pittsburgh) and the head of the ATF office in Pittsburgh, Corky James, sat on his left.

The Attorney General sifted through a pile of e-mails and letters stacked on the desk in front of him. He had been getting pressure from various members of Congress and from highly placed military officers about the way the Mulhaney case was being handled. The Congressmen were complaining that some of their constituents were at the point of rebellion. The military was concerned at the direction this prosecution might be headed - the confiscation of all weapons. They were worried that they might face mutiny if soldiers were ordered to seize civilian weapons. The whole question was why the BATF had to be so heavy handed. At the top of the stack of paper was a letter from the CIA, requesting that the Attorney General intervene in the Mulhaney prosecution.

Carnegie skimmed through the CIA's letter again and said, "I have a document here that claims you received a warning before your agent got shot. I don't recall ever seeing that in any reports."

Corky James, the BATF man from Pittsburgh, said, "Well, Sir, we're really not sure the warning was legitimate."

"Do you know someone named Sam Budda?"

"He's the bozo who came to us with this story about being hired by someone who was going to start shooting agents," James said.

"Did you listen to what he had to say?" the Attorney General said.

"We put him under investigation and tapped his phones."

"Under investigation for what?"

"For obstructing justice, interfering in a federal investigation, whatever. . . .," James said.

"For Christ's sake man, he comes to you with this warning and you investigate him. Why?"

"I just saw him as a kook, Sir."

"Didn't occur to you to work with him? See what you could learn? Figure out some way to avoid what he was telling you?"

"No sir, it didn't. He's just a wise-ass who hates cops and was wasting our time."

"I probably missed something," Bunker-Jones said, "but I thought one of your agents was killed after Budda warned you that would happen."

"Oh, yes, sir. An agent was killed. But we don't know that his killing has anything to do with this," James said.

"Wasn't the dead agent found with a copy of the letter sent to the Post Gazette stuffed in his shirt?"

"Yes. But that could have been a copy."

"How so? The letter wasn't published."

"Sir, the gun nut who wrote this empty threat could have passed it around to his nutty friends, and one of them may have killed the agent."

"Well if that's true, Mr. James," Bunker-Jones said acidly, "it hardly helps your point, does it. In either case, someone who doesn't like what you did to Mulhaney shot your agent. What difference does it make if it's the person who wrote the letter or not?"

"I guess I didn't think of that, Sir."

At length the Attorney General said, "Let's get to the underlying problem here, the Mulhaney case. I've never understood one thing, Agent James, what is the purpose of using a paramilitary force when the ATF wants to arrest somebody?"

"Sir," James said, "it's pretty simple. These people want to kill us, so we go in with enough force to keep that from happening."

Ainsworth Bunker-Jones, said, "Had Mulhaney made threats? Is that why you think he wanted to kill you?"

"No sir."

"What then?" Bunker-Jones continued. "He was asleep when you came into his house. Just how much of a threat was he?"

"That's just it, Sir. We go when they're asleep so they can't kill us."

"Had you thought of knocking on the door?" Carnegie asked.

"Too dangerous, Sir," the ATF man said.

"Too dangerous to knock on the door," Carnegie said. "Whatever happened to the time when one or two agents went into the worst situations, even to arrest a known felon?"

"Those times are past, Sir. We don't do it that way any more."

"So I gather, Mr. James. But the question is why," Carnegie pressed.

"We don't want our agents to be killed, Sir."

"Is there any limit to this caution of yours, Mr. James?" Bunker-Jones said.

"What do you mean, Sir?"

"Well if you're afraid of dying . . . "

"We're not afraid, Sir. . . "

"If you're afraid of dying," Bunker-Jones repeated, "why not use machine guns or rocket propelled grenades to soften up the suspect before you go in? Hopefully, you would do this without killing too many of the neighbors. The people you want to arrest would be frightened into submission and no agents would be endangered."

"We didn't kill anyone, sir."

"No," Bunker-Jones said. "Thank God. You just terrorized three little boys, broke Mulhaney's jaw and knocked his wife unconscious. Sorry I misspoke."

"Begging your pardon, Sir, but whose side are you on?"

"Not yours," Bunker-Jones shot back.

"Here's the bottom line Agent James," Carnegie said. "Your posturing with twenty some odd men dressed in black battle gear and invading a suburban house with guns drawn, is causing this office no end of trouble, both on and off Capitol Hill. And given what you were up against, an ordinary man with a wife and a family, sound asleep, I don't know what else to say about your actions except that they were goddam irresponsible and adolescent."

Carnegie let the word adolescent sink in. "It's our view here that if you and the people in your office cannot conduct yourselves professionally and with consideration and courtesy to ordinary citizens, you're in the wrong line of work. And I don't call jack-booted thuggery courteous."

James' color rose and he squirmed. Ms. Adams, the United States Attorney for Pittsburgh, shrank in her seat.

"Now we need to. . ."

"Begging your pardon, Sir," James interrupted, "We won the case. Our conduct can't have been too bad."

"Mr. James," he said, "when the federal government puts its imprimatur on a case, the man in the street believes the person charged is guilty. And so he is more likely to convict that acquit. Additionally, and I was going to get to this later, I believe your people made some discreet inquiries into the backgrounds of some or all of the jurors."

"Well, yes, sir. We always do that. We need to know who we're dealing with."

"Were you aware of this Ms. Adams?" Bunker-Jones asked.

"No, this is the first I've heard of it."

Carnegie said, "Well, Mr. James, if you were serving on the jury and you discovered the same guys in Black suits who broke Mulhaney's jaw and terrorized his family were asking around about you, how would you vote on the case?"

"I guess I never thought of it that way," James said.

"Seems like there is a lot of that going around," Bunker-Jones said.

"All right," Carnegie said, "Let's get down to it. We are here because we need to map a strategy for damage control. We've . . . "

"Begging your pardon, Sir, but what damage?"

"Hasn't an agent had been killed and aren't the people responsible promising to kill more agents?"

Bunker-Jones and Carnegie exchanged looks. Adams fidgeted.

Carnegie said, "Mr. James, thank you for your participation in this conference and for taking time to fly to Washington to meet with us. If you would wait in the outer office, Ms. Adams will be with you shortly."

James got up without a word and left the room. When he was gone, Carnegie turned to Adams and said, "Why in the hell did you prosecute this case in the first place?"

"I was told it was an important case. It involved a machine gun."

"It involved a semi-automatic rifle, legally purchased and legally possessed, that malfunctioned and was in need of repair," Bunker-Jones said.

"It involved guns, sir. I don't like guns. They scare me," Adams said.

Carnegie and Bunker-Jones again exchanged looks.

"Guns scare you so you prosecute a case where there is no case?" Carnegie said.

"I wouldn't say there is no case, Sir. The statute says you may not possess a machine gun, and he had one. I thought you and the party organization would be pleased because I was doing my part to stamp out guns. In fact, I thought the president didn't like guns."

"This isn't the anti-gun lobby, Ms. Adams. This is the Justice Department. We don't pursue openly political agendas here. We seek justice," Carnegie said, somewhat heatedly.

"Well, I thought I had done that, Sir."

"Were you at all concerned about the fact that Mulhaney hadn't had a chance to have the gun repaired, that he was not trying to hide anything, or that twenty-two men dressed in battle gear stormed his house and terrorized his family in the dead of night?" Bunker-Jones said.

"Well, no, Sir. I wasn't concerned. He had possession of the gun and no one knows when or if he would have gotten it fixed. And as for the family, I don't get into that. The ATF runs its own operations."

"And when you looked into this guy Mulhaney," Carnegie said, "did it seem like he was the radical type? Someone who would never get the gun fixed?"

"I didn't speculate on that, Sir."

"But we speculate all the time, don't we," Bunker-Jones said. "We consider who it is we are dealing with, and that's part of the decision whether or not to prosecute. Here we've got a young guy with a steady job and a family, a veteran. Unless you wanted to break his balls, why wouldn't you wait a couple weeks, knock on the door, and ask to see the rifle. If he wouldn't show it to you, why wouldn't you then simply obtain a warrant and knock on the door again?

"As I said, Sir, I don't get into how ATF does things."

"Well, we're sure as hell in the thick of how they do things now, aren't we?" Carnegie said.

9

Three weeks passed after the killing of the ATF agent, and the bureau had made no move to relax its position on the Mulhaney case. Neither the Attorney General nor the BATF had been in touch with Sam. This wasn't altogether unexpected, and the old men decided to move into phase two of their plan.

Aaron owned a Chevrolet 3500 van. It had no windows in the back except for two eighteen-inch square windows in the double doors. Aaron took the van to a neighborhood body shop, where he had the rear door windows refitted. Originally, they were fixed in position. Aaron specified that the new windows snap on the tracks.

While the van was in the body shop, Aaron was busy in his shop constructing a heavy bench for shooting. It was made of two by fours and three-quarter inch plywood, and it had a flat table top on which to rest a rifle and an attached seat. When it was completed, Aaron invited Jamie and Jesse over to help with the installation.

Together, they lifted the bench into the back of the van and secured it against the driver's side of the truck with bolts and with two sided tape. The tape was stronger than the bolts and the bench may as well have been welded to the frame. It was positioned near the rear doors, with just enough clearance to lower the window in front of the bench. The height was perfect for a rifle resting on heavy sandbags against the fore-end and underneath the stock, creating a rock-solid shooting position.

When the fastening of the bench was completed and it was determined that the windows could be lowered with the bench in place, Aaron went into the house and came out with a Seiko .30-06 bolt gun. Jamie placed two large leather sandbags on the bench and Aaron got into the back of the truck with the rifle and lowered it onto the sandbags. The rifle's muzzle sat six inches above the bottom of the window and three inches inside the open window. The rifle itself rested securely on the heavy sandbags. Aaron had built the seat exactly to his height, and he leaned easily over the bench, tucking the butt plate and the sandbag firmly into his shoulder with the sandbag actually holding the rifle in place, and grasping the fore-end with his left hand. With the rifle in position and his cheek on the stock, he sighted through the scope. The shooting position was ideal and it was steady.

"Pretty nifty," Jamie admired.

"There's gonna be a hell of a blast inside the truck," Aaron said.

"That's what ear muffs are for," Jamie said.

The next morning, the three eighty year olds were up and moving early. Jesse drove a Lincoln Navigator, Jamie Berenger drove a Toyota Tundra pickup truck, and Aaron drove his Chevrolet van. They met at six a.m. at the Sunrise Café in Lawrenceville on Butler Street. Talk was subdued over the breakfast special of three eggs, toast, bacon and potatoes. At 6:30 sharp, the three men left the restaurant and went to their respective cars. Aaron and Jesse headed back toward town on Butler Street. Jamie went the other direction on Butler, toward Aspinwall.

For some weeks Jamie had monitored the movements of Corky James, the head of station for the BATF in Pittsburgh. Aaron and Jesse had objected to this on the grounds that James might be heavily guarded and Jamie might be discovered. But Jamie insisted. "We know this fucker is gonna stonewall and put his men at risk. He ought'a be at risk," he said.

Although James' movements could not be monitored once he entered the federal building garage, Jamie trailed him as he left his house in the mornings and again as he left the federal building in the evenings. James left his Fox Chapel house at seven o'clock. In the evening, his movements were irregular. Sometimes he left work at five o'clock. Sometimes not until nine. Once he got home from work, he never went out again until the next morning,

Today, James pulled out of his driveway at 7:02 a.m. and headed for Route 28 and downtown Pittsburgh. Jamie Berenger saw the BATF man leave and then broke off surveillance and dialed Jesse on his cell phone. "He just left."

Jesse dialed Aaron and said, "He's on his way." Both Jesse and Aaron were already in place. Jesse was parked on Butler Street. Normally, James would cross over the 40th Street Bridge, turn onto Butler Street, and drive right past Jesse's position. But today, Jesse pulled out in front of the BATF car as it approached. Today, things would be different.

At seven twenty-five, Aaron 's Bluetooth rang and Jesse said, "Here we come. I just pulled out in front of him. He's following me. I'm just now turning onto Main Street. He's right behind me. We're starting up the hill toward you."

Aaron was in position just up the hill that James and the BATF man were ascending. Surveillance over the last weeks established that James traveled up Main Street every morning and made the obligatory stop at the intersection of Main and Davison.

Today Aaron sat Davison Street, forty yards from the intersection where James would stop, with the back of the van pointed toward the intersection.

Aaron put down his cell phone and put on his ear muffs. James was only a few seconds away. He leaned forward and released the catches on the rear window of the left door. It slid down its track and created an opening in the truck's rear door where the window would have been. Aaron hunched into the seat on the shooting bench and hunkered down with the rifle tucked into his shoulder and the reticle of the four-power Zeiss scope on the middle of the intersection forty yards distant.

Jesse's Lincoln Navigator came into view and stopped at the corner of Main and Davison, headed up the hill that was Main Street. Jesse glanced left and saw that the van was parked forty yards down Davison with the rear doors facing him and the shooting window down. James stopped his gray government sedan close to the Navigator's bumper, apparently angry that Jesse had pulled in front of him a block earlier.

"Perfect," Aaron said to himself.

The intersection was clear of cars and the Lincoln Navigator pulled out slowly, so slowly that it almost seemed something was wrong with the car. When the Navigator's rear bumper was in the middle of the intersection, James' Ford sedan had begun to move, and then Jesse stopped altogether. James jammed on the brakes, stopping inches from the Lincoln Navigator's rear bumper and blew the horn.

That was his last act. A .30-06 armour piercing round entered just above his left ear and exited near the crown of his head, continuing on through the passenger window and down Davison Street another three hundred yards, where it embedded itself in the trunk of an oak tree in Arsenal Park.

James' body was thrown violently to the right and lay slumped across the console onto the passenger seat, his arms at his sides. The top of his head was missing, and blood covered the passenger compartment of the car, forming an opaque coating on part of the windscreen and the passenger window, which was perfectly in tact except for a small hole where the .30-caliber round pierced the glass, traveling at 2800 feet per second on its way to Arsenal Park.

Jesse heard the report of the rifle and immediately accelerated up Main Street toward Penn Avenue. Behind him, the Ford sedan sat in the intersection. Aaron raised the back window into the closed position and secured the rifle in a metal case. He moved to the driver's seat and was starting the van when he looked in the rear view mirror and saw a man get out of a car behind James' Ford and walk up toward the driver's door. Aaron was pulling out when he saw the man gesture wildly with his hands and run back to his car.

Aaron's van pulled out slowly and continued down Davison. Cars were beginning to stack up behind the gray sedan stalled in the intersection.

10

The Central Intelligence Agency. Langley, Virginia. Two days after Corky James, the Chief ATF Agent in the Pittsburgh office, was killed.

John Corbett, Director of Central Intelligence sat in a leather armchair sipping coffee. Across from him were two other men, James Ferriter, Deputy Director Research, and Gregory Naratova, Deputy Director and Chief of Operations.

Corbett said, "I recently received a confidential communication from the Attorney General concerning this Mulhaney case that has been much in the newspapers lately. The gist of it is that Congress is on the A.G.'s back to get rid of the case because their constituents are going nuts, but he can't discontinue the prosecution because he's stuck with the President's anti-gun policy. The President wants the case to go forward and he doesn't care about the public outcry. The way the President sees it, more people support him than oppose him.

"Even before I got the AG's memo, I had been somewhat concerned about this thing and so I asked two of Gregory's analysts to look it at the situation. In a nutshell, they seem to think this could develop into something that might affect the survival of this agency and maybe even the government. I'll let you explain it Gregory."

Naratova said, "For fifty years, we have been successful promoting the image of the United States as a democratic utopia, where little guys become president and anyone can get rich and fair play and decency are the order of the day. This disinformation campaign is designed to keep the lid on things. If everything is great, there's no reason to rebel, and in any case, our own financial relationships with the large multi-national corporations are kept hidden."

"So how does that relate to the Pittsburgh thing?" Ferriter said.

"We promote the government as benign, but if the gun nuts- or whoever is killing these ATF agents--are able to make a case that BATF's Reynolds trooper tactics are the true face of government, people who are already disaffected by left wing politics and the steady downturn of the economy may begin to rebel, resulting in a collapse of the economy and the government itself."

"You've got to be joking," Ferriter said.

"Suppose the average guy begins to think the government he's always believed in is likely to kick his door in and wreck his house. Suppose he thinks this is not an unusual event, but is the way government conducts business, and that in order to quell resistance, the government is gearing up to take everyone's guns," Naratova said.

"That's stupid. No one would think that," Ferriter said.

Naratova said, "why is it stupid? BATF is the government, it's kicking doors in as its normal way of doing business, and it's seizing guns in the process."

"All right," Ferriter said, "let's start from square one. We promote the idea that American citizens live in a democracy where everyone has a chance and the government is benevolent and voting decides elections. So far so good. And then BATF comes along and demonstrates that government isn't so benevolent. That presents a problem for us. But let's keep it in perspective. I don't see the BATF's misconduct as creating all that many risks."

Corbett said, "We don't always know what risks we are creating. Remember when in the late 1950s corporations were flexing their muscles and were pressuring Congress to put us under stricter controls with oversight committees? We hadn't yet worked out a financial relationship with the big corporations. Remember our response to their blustering? We forged several partnerships with key Congressional leaders and we invented the Red scare.

"Then McCarthy took our bright idea and ran with it. He went around the countryside terrorizing everybody and the corporations had to keep their heads down and didn't have time to concentrate on us. Nobody wanted to be accused of being a communist. So our disinformation was just what we'd hoped for, until we began to question if we could control McCarthy. We failed to predict that he would have his own ideas about who should be president. That was a risk we hadn't foreseen. And it was a hell of a big one."

"Yeah, but we kept it under control, ultimately." Ferriter said.

"Yes, but I'm convinced this situation is even more volatile. I'm not sure we can control the fallout, " Corbett said.

"Why?" Ferriter said.

"We can and we have created a fury over communists or a fear that abortion is ungodly or an outrage that affirmative action isn't working, and the effect is confusion and anger. But middle America isn't really affected by these things. Joe Sixpack likes to posture about them, but he doesn't really care. On the other hand, when our government starts breaking into Joe's house and taking away his only means of self-defense, we suddenly have an explosive situation."

"Not only that, but we've got record unemployment and we've got left-wing politicians threatening to do everything from taking guns to shutting down talk radio. We're at a flash point."

"Why does BATF need to operate a paramilitary army anyway?" Ferriter said.

"They use the paramilitary army to make the case that what they do is dangerous," Naratova said. "It must be dangerous or they wouldn't need to use an army. Catch-22. "

"You mean this is driven by trying to get a bigger budget?" Ferriter said.

"Yes. But the irony is they've already got huge funding and they've created symbiotic relationships with a slew of anti-gun Congressmen who keep the money flowing," Corbett said.

"Then how does this make any sense?"

"You have to remember," Naratova said, " They're stupid. Worse, they're power hungry. This new director is trying to build an empire."

"But even if you're right, the general public doesn't seem to be too upset over this. In fact, a jury convicted this Mulhaney."

Naratova said, "The analysts feel the only way to account for this verdict is that almost everyone on that jury was afraid of reprisals if they acquitted."

"Reprisals from the government?" Corbet said.

"Who else? We uncovered BATF investigations on all of the jurors. The jurors knew this because the BATF made sure they knew it. We're just now finding out that BATF also leaned on some of the witnesses. When the gun nuts find this out, they will argue-correctly-- that the government not only brutalizes people for exercising the right of self-defense, but it also corrupts the judicial system by terrorizing juries. At that point, we risk large numbers of average people joining them. And our disinformation about the kind and sympathetic government is out the window."

"So what? What can people do? They might not like it, but they're not going to start shooting up the government," Ferriter said.

"According to our analysts, the most likely responses would be refusals to pay taxes, mass demonstrations, calls for resignation and impeachment, and increasingly severe confrontations with police. A third political party would be likely to arise and bill itself as a reformer. At some point, the government might actually fail."

"Now we have reached my concern," Corbet said. "Should new parties take control, our operations and even our existence could be in jeopardy. I don't want that to happen."

"If BATF had been smart," Corbet continued, "it would have just quietly built itself a luxurious little niche at taxpayer expense. It could have made a few quiet arrests to keep civilization safe from guns, but allowed most people to keep their guns along with the illusion of being able to use those guns against us, the government, should we get out of line."

"What do you mean, illusion," Ferriter said. "You just said that there was a real threat to government."

"I guess I should have said that while there is a threat from guns, the more immediate threat is from non-cooperation and civil disobedience leading to the formation of a third political party. The threat is from getting rid of the corrupt relationships that we have built over the years. That is the most likely threat to the existing government," Corbet said.

"Where does this leave us?" Ferriter asked.

"We need to limit the damage these clowns in BATF are doing and deflect the poplar reaction to their stupidity," Corbet said. "We have a problem that could easily get out of hand. I want you to map out a plan to deal with this, Gregory."

"Right now the problem is still localized in Pittsburgh. I think the planning ought to be done there with people familiar with that territory. We have two retired operatives in Pittsburgh. I might contact them and ask them to work with me on this," Naratova said.

"Budda and Savarese?" Ferriter said.

"Yes. They've been reasonably effective in other operations."

"Budda is a loose-cannon killer," Ferriter said emphatically. "You aren't forgetting that he shot two men in my section during the last assignment he had with us."

"Aren't you forgetting," Naratova said, "that he shot them because your men were dirty?"

"Look," Corbet said, "I know Budda's unpredictable, but right now he may be just what we need."

"How so?" Ferriter said.

Corbet said, "I want ATF to no longer be in a position to threaten the continued viability of this agency, and I don't care what it takes to accomplish that, including killing every jack-booted sonofabitch over there. Doing this may require all the violence that Sam Budda can bring to bear."

11

Sam Budda often worked as a private contractor for federal agencies. He had been hired by the CIA to look into the murders of seven CIA agents in Iraq between 2002 and 2004. During that time, there were more civilian contractors in Iraq than military personnel. The civilian contractors provided security for the military itself as well as for diplomats, repaired aircraft and heavy equipment, trained Iraqi police, helped to set up an Iraqi civil government, wrote laws, created bureaucracies, staffed hospitals, built barracks, repaired the infrastructure, provided food service, and in the course of doing so, collected fees costing literally billions of tax dollars.

Sam sat in Gregory Naratova's office at CIA headquarters at Langley, Virginia. As the Chief of Operations, Naratova occupied a sumptuous corner office overlooking rolling hills, a meandering creek and patches of Virginia woods. The men sipped coffee as they talked, seated near large windows at the end of the room opposite Naratova's desk.

"How were these agents killed?" Sam said.

"Four were killed by roadside bombs and three were shot with long-range rifles," Naratova said.

"What makes you think there is anything unusual about these killings? Isn't that what often happens to Americans who work in Iraq?"

"We don't normally lose this many agents anywhere. Our people are trained to be careful."

"It's hard to be careful of a roadside bomb," Sam said.

"I know," Naratova answered.

"What were these agents working on?" Sam casually asked.

Naratova sat as if he were frozen in position. His eyes shifted to Sam.

"What?" Sam said, puzzled.

"Jesus Christ. Stupid. It's right there in front of me. They were working on what virtually every agent in Iraq is working on-how much the civilian contractors are stealing and how they are doing it."

"Who is hunting terrorists like Osama Bin Laden if you guys are all looking for crooks?"

"Army Intelligence, Navy Intelligence, Marine Intelligence, and every Special Operations group in existence including the goddam FBI," Naratova said, "not to mention the CIA in every other country in the world."

"O.K. everybody else is looking for terrorists and the CIA in Iraq is looking for crooks. What's so special about the crooks in Iraq?" Sam said.

"It's not the crooks," Naratova said. "It's the money. Hundreds of billions, Sam. The contractors in Iraq are literally bigger than the U.S. government there. We downsized the military decades ago, but when you fight a war, you have the same supply needs, the same security needs, the same medical needs whether you're downsized or not, so you hire private contractors to do the stuff that the military cannot do."

"And theft is rampant," Sam ventured.

"That's an understatement," Naratova said.

"I'll venture one more guess," Sam said.

"What?"

"I'll bet these contractors are full of retired state department and military guys. They might even have one or two spooks," Sam said.

"You're right," Naratova said.

Sam started to get up. "Well, there you have it. You don't need me," he said. He returned the highly decorated Russian china coffee cup to its saucer as he stood. "Your mystery is solved. Just like always. Follow the money."

"Sit down," Naratova said. "The fact that I didn't see what was in front of my face means I need you more than I thought I did."

"You must have some of your own people working on this," Sam said.

"Yes, a whole team. But they're not my people. I'm spread too thin. This team reports to Jim Ferriter," Naratova said.

"You gotta wonder why a team of seasoned operatives didn't see the obvious," Sam said.

* * *

After Sam came on board, he got unprecedented power to initiate wire taps and conduct any sort of investigation he saw fit to undertake. Sam was required to work with two men of the six who had worked on the murders before he got there, Dirkin and La Scola. They worked for Sam but they also reported to Ferriter.

After arriving in Baghdad, Sam kept Ferriter's men busy with nonsense and did virtually all the investigative work himself.

Baghdad was like a huge mixmaster running at full speed in the middle of the desert. People were coming and going and life seemed move at a pace that made New York look slow. But it wasn't New York. It was the wild west in the Middle East. Cowboys and tough guys were all over and everybody was making six figures. Contractors and military personnel were swirling around each other in a lethal mix of war, money and profiteering.

The contractors drove around in armored Mercedes, tricked-out Humvees, and exotic motorcycles. They often traveled in motorcades protected by trucks mounted with machine guns. It was as if the contractors were celebrities in a movie set.

Although Sam had an office in the CIA complex, he was seldom there, much to the consternation of Ferriter's men, who couldn't keep track of him. Sam had a safe house in the Green Zone with a secure line to Langley. There he studied printouts of who was getting paid for what. Based on the reports of the murdered agents, his attention was drawn to a medical supplier, a communications repair contractor, and an aviation service.

When he checked the personnel rosters of government contractors in Iraq and Afghanistan, these three were the only contractors with ex-CIA agents as employees. He linked all six of the Ferriter team who had worked on the murders with the ex-CIA men now employed as contractors. Using his authority to install wiretaps, a special team was sent in to set up and monitor the phones of the ex-CIA men.

Within a few days, conversations were intercepted and recorded with thinly veiled references to the murders of the CIA agents. One of Ferriter's men stationed in Iraq with Sam was recorded on a call to the former agent then working for the communications company.

"Jensen," he said, "this is Dirkin."

"Dirkin," Jensen said. "What's up?"

"I'm getting a little worried about this guy we told you about."

"Yeah, this hot-shot hired gun. Sherlock Holmes. I thought I'd hear from him by now," Jensen said. "But he hasn't been anywhere near the company as far as I can tell. What are you concerned about?"

"I don't know what the hell he's doing. He's up to something, but we don't know what. We don't even know where he is most of the time, and he has us doing dumb stuff."

"How about I talk to Jimmy and we set up a roadside bomb or something for Mr. Sleuth?"

"I was hoping you'd say that. I think we better do it sooner than later."

After Jensen ended his conversation with Dirkin, Ferriter's man, he called Jimmy Burl at the medical supply contractor.

"Jimmy, this is Jensen. Just got a call from Dirkin. He thinks that guy we got a memo about is maybe getting a little dangerous."

"What's he doing?"

"That's just it. They don't know. They also don't know where he is most of the time and he's got them doing shitwork. Has he showed up at your outfit?"

"No. Anthony ain't seen him either at the airlines."

"Dirkin and La Scola want us to blow him up. What do you think?"

"Hell yeah, why not? Why take chances? But why not just have Dirkin and La Scola pop him? They work with him."

"Nah. They need to be seen in a restaurant somewhere when this happens," Jensen said. "Talk to Anthony. Tell him to use the same guys as the last time."

"Yeah. Okay. Christ, I don't think they even found his teeth last time," Jimmy said.

Sam reviewed the tapes daily and was aware that his death was imminent. On a secure line to Naratova:

"Hello Naratova, Sam here."

"Hello Sam. How are things in the desert?"

"Looks like Ferriter's guys are dirty, at the least the two that you sent with me, and the three ex-ops working for as contractors are not only dirty, but they are the ones that killed your boys."

"Why'd they kill them?"

"I can only speculate that your guys were closing in on their scams, so they killed them. I don't have any idea what the scams are. All I know is they killed your agents. I'm sending you the tapes."

"What about Dirkin and La Scola?"

"They're in it too. My guess is they feed the contractors inside information and stall any internal investigations that might get too close. They already set me up. The contractors are setting up a roadside bomb for my amusement."

"What are they doing that they need to kill CIA agents?"

"All I know is that the three corporations scored almost a billion dollars last year."

"All right," Naratova said. "I'll get a team on it right away. We'll tear those fuckers apart. They've taken their last billion. We'll find out what they're doing. They'll wish they never got in the contractor business before this is over."

"What do you want me to do on this end?" Sam said.

"You figure it out," Naratova said.

"My man," Sam said. "Talk to you."

That afternoon, Sam went out to a rifle range with three of the agents who operated his wiretaps. They ran through standard close range handgun and subgun exercises and after two hours, Sam was satisfied he could count on these men in a fight.

The next morning, he called Dirkin and La Scola.

"Dirkin, this is Sam. I need you and La Scola right now."

"Where are you?"

"I'm in an apartment in Khulani Square."

"How do we get there?"

"Take the Al Jumhuriya Bridge across the river and turn left on Khulfafa Street."

"O.K. That's near the bus station, isn't it?"

"Yeah. Go a few blocks to Khulani Square. I'm at number 27."

"Be right there. Do we need rifles?"

"No. Strictly surveillance."

Once across the Jumhuriya Bridge, Ferriter's men would be out of the Green Zone, or the International Zone, as it is sometimes called, and in Baghdad at large. There they would encounter traffic that was either gridlocked or snarled, and by the time they got to his apartment, they would be worn out and disoriented.

The Americans had suspended the authority of Iraqi traffic police some months earlier, and the result was that stolen cars flooded into Baghdad from all over Europe and the Middle East. No police checked the ownership papers of the cars or driving licenses, and Baghdad quickly became a tangle of unlicensed drivers in stolen cars banging into anything near the street and scraping past each other in an enthusiastic show of what it was like to drive in the new democracy. The only vehicles that got through this mess with any degree of success were Humvees mounted with .50 caliber machine guns. They simply plowed over the hoods of cars that got in the way.

Although the distance from the CIA offices to Sam's apartment in Khulani Square was only a few miles, it took Ferriter's men nearly two hours to get there.

"Come in," Sam said, in response to a knock. He was seated on a couch twenty feet away, facing the door, a newspaper on his lap, covering the Para Ordinance P-14 .45-caliber pistol in his right hand.

Dirkin opened the door almost gingerly, and hesitated before entering.

"Come on in," Sam motioned with his left hand.

Dirkin walked in with La Scola behind, and as La Scola reached to close the door, a hand grabbed his wrist, twisted it behind his back, jerked him off balance to the right, and knocked him to the floor. One of Sam's operatives had been hiding behind the open door.

Reaching for his gun, Dirkin pivoted toward the man on top of his sprawling colleague. He froze when he saw Sam's .45-caliber pistol pointed at his head. Two men emerged with short sub-guns, one from a room behind Sam and one from a room to the left of the door. Both had their guns trained on Durkin. He raised his hands and the man nearest him disarmed him and patted him down, removing a small hideout gun from a coat pocket.

Both CIA rogues were forced to kneel in front of Sam, who remained in the couch with the .45 pointed vaguely in their direction. One of the operatives stood behind Sam. The other two stood behind the men on the floor.

"What do you want?" Durkin said.

"I want you to call your three colleagues at Mason Aviation, Dynex Communications, and Hicks Medical and get them over here right now. Tell them it is an emergency. It's 27 Khulani Square, in case you forgot."

"And if I don't?"

There was a muzzle flash two feet from Durkin's head and a tidal wave of sound ripped through his head, leaving his ears ringing in reaction to the explosion. In a movement that no one saw, Sam had raised his gun and shot La Scola in the head. The 230 grain .45 caliber full metal jacket bullet entered his forehead at the junction of the nose and exited the back of his head in a spray of blood and brain matter. La Scola's body jerked and sprawled backwards on the floor, his feet tucked under him.

Durkin gasped for breath as his hand jerked involuntarily to his mouth, terror overwhelming his face.

"I....I.....I.....," he stammered.

"Would you like to live?" Sam said..

Durkin, drenched in a fear induced sweat, shook his head in the affirmative, stammering with manic enthusiasm that he could not control.

"Then you need to make those calls," Sam said. "We'll take a minute for you to calm yourself, then you'll get on the phone. Franz, drag La Scola's body out of here, will you?"

One of Sam's agents dragged La Scola by his feet into the next room.

Within two hours, all three of the former CIA men walked through the door at 27 Khulani Square. Each was unceremoniously knocked to the floor and bound with duct tape.

When the men were secured, Sam took a walk around the block. He wanted to make sure none of the men had been followed or left associates outside. He left the four rogue agents on the floor in the company of his agents while he sat in an outdoor café across the street from the apartment drinking a chilled Pellegrino and glancing through the headlines of a local paper.

Satisfied the operation was clear, he returned to the apartment and looked at the bound men scattered on the floor. Selecting the most belligerent looking of the group, Sam sat him up against the couch, and ripped the tape off his mouth. The man glared at him.

"What's your name," Sam said.

"Go fuck yourself," the man said.

"Wrong answer," Sam said. "Strike one."

"Who do you work for?"

The man stared steadily into Sam's eyes. He was struggling to put up a good show, but he could smell death in the room. Warnings erupted like neon signs flashing. He didn't want to die. He could tell Sam where he worked. There was no harm in that. Maybe that would placate him. "Mason Aviation," he said.

"Very good, Mr. Fuck Yourself," Sam said. "How is Mason scamming on its contract?"

The man said nothing. Sam unholstered his .45 and pointed it at the man's head. Off to the side, Durkin started squirming and grunting under his duct tape. The man looked at Durkin and saw abject fear. He looked back at Sam, who regarded him levelly.

"All right. We put in used parts. We buy them all over Europe and the States and we paint them up and put them in boxes so they look new, and we sell them to the government as new."

"What else?"

"The usual. We bill for a lot of stuff we never do."

"What else?"

"If we aren't going twenty-four hours a day, the mechanics will break stuff on the helicopters so they'll have to come in sooner for work."

"How much more do you make by doing this stuff?" Sam said.

"It's about a factor of twenty. So if we should bill a million, we do twenty million."

"Why'd you kill the CIA agents?" Sam said.

"Now wait a minute. These guys were our friends."

"I know you killed them. Were they getting too close?"

The man looked at Dirkin, who nodded nervously. Sweat poured from his forehead into his eyes. The duct tape puffed in and out as he tried to breathe through his mouth.

"They were asking for invoices and stuff like that."

"Didn't you expect that?"

"Hell no. Not in a war zone. We expected them to go along and get along. Nobody would say they weren't doing their jobs."

Sam stood up and shot the man in the face. He clicked the safety on the .45, holstered the weapon, opened the door to the apartment, and walked out into the hall and down the stairs to the lobby.

As he exited the building, he heard the staccato of the submachine guns. No more CIA agents would be killed by these contractors.

12

Sam Budda leaned on the railing of the Grandview Avenue overlook. The vista included the Monongahela and the Allegheny rivers, coming together at the tip of a geographic triangle, to form the Ohio. At the apex of the triangle was a large fountain shooting water fifty feet into the air. Toward town from the fountain was Point State Park, a large grassy area that includes the remains of Fort Pitt, a colonial fort that guarded the joining of the waters. Behind Point State Park was downtown Pittsburgh itself, punctuated by modern skyscrapers and brightly colored neon signs on the sides of tall buildings. The signs advertised banks, brokerage firms and large insurance companies. The old Gulf tower, around since the days when Gulf Oil was the third largest oil company in the world, was illuminated in white, blue or red, the different colors signaling a change in the weather. Tugboats churned the rivers, going in both directions with their barges. Cars crossed the bridges up and down the rivers, coming out of and going into town.

Gregory Naratova stood next to Sam Budda on the overlook. Sam was dressed in a gray Filson wool Mackinaw, Naratova in a tan overcoat and baseball cap. They both stared out at the vista before them.

"Now let me get this straight," Sam snorted, "you want me to save the CIA from the BATF."

"That's a somewhat uncharitable way to put it," Naratova said.

"You put it another way," Sam said.

"We want you to end the viability of ATF as an agency and we want you to keep a lid on the incipient rebellion that is being fueled by whoever is shooting ATF agents."

"And how do I do that?"

"To begin with, you could find out who is doing it."

"Funny you should mention that. I'm already working for the guy who's doing the killing. He hired me to represent him to ATF."

Naratova pushed off the railing and stared at Sam, his mouth open. After a pause, he said, "You've got to be joking. You know who it is?"

"No, I don't know who he is. I've never met him. He sent Nick and me a money order through the mail and asked us to serve as his messenger to ATF. I've talked to him on the phone and I've delivered a couple of messages to ATF. That's all."

"What were the messages?"

"The first was that he would start killing agents if they didn't publish his letter to the Post Gazette. The other was that he was going to kill them if they didn't back off Mulhaney."

"Why did he need you for that?"

"That's what I asked him. He said he wanted some outside person to know exactly what he had told ATF so they couldn't cover it up-at least not without killing me."

"What else did he say?"

"Nothing."

"Do you have any idea who the shooter is?"

"None. The voice on the phone was modulated with some electronic device. I don't have a clue."

"The Director wants you to find out and put a stop to this."

"This guy is paying me to help him muscle the BATF and you want to pay me to muscle him. What's behind this, anyway?" Sam said. "There has never been any love between the agency and the BATF."

"The director is concerned that the Mulhaney foolishness coupled with the killing ATF agents, will start a landslide of rebellion that will go out of control."

"Does that really seem likely?"

"I know you're familiar with our disinformation techniques."

"Yes. I've seen them applied."

"A by-product of disinformation is always confusion and anger, an explosive combination. We are concerned that our disinformation-that government is your friend although it may do a few things you don't like-will conflict with the message of ATF-that government is a jack booted thug. And when our message collides with that of ATF, we expect major problems."

"Interesting. You're saying the population is at a flash point, in part because of the mix of disinformation that you and the ATF have been shoveling out for years?"

"Yes, it's a complex calculation. We not only have to factor in the disinformation, but also what has been happening in the economy and in politics in recent years. In a nutshell, the economy is going south for a good many people, and those people are joining the ranks of libertarian types who are increasingly fed up with the left wing direction of the country. This is epitomized in those bumper stickers you see all over- "The Socialist States of America." Our analysts are telling us we may have reached an explosive mix if this latest stuff goes any farther than it has."

"But you're part of the problem too," Sam said. "You've had a part in creating this explosive mix with all that crap you've been making up for years?"

"That's true."

"Chickens will come home," Sam mused. "Surely you are not thinking of an armed rebellion."

"Not unless this killing of ATF agents gets out of control. More likely is a political rebellion and the demise of the two party system. That is the perceived threat to our security."

"Right now the political parties are controlled by you and the corporations, so new parties present an unknown that is likely to be difficult to manage. Is that it?" Sam said.

"Yes."

"Why not just assign a truckload of your people to find this shooter, shut him down, and you're done."

"You and I have seen this before, Sam. Sometimes a single person can accomplish more than a battalion."

"Under your scenario, one or two people would find the shooter, persuade him to stop killing ATF agents, and the problem would go away."

"Not exactly. The ATF would still be there doing the same stuff it has always done, and therefore, presenting us with the same difficulty we have now. We need them to stop doing that," Naratova said.

"That's funny. That's who they are. They'll never stop doing that. They're thugs and overreachers. They're what they always have been. You want to take the spots off the leopard."

"If that's what it takes, that's what the director wants you to do," Naratova said.

Sam turned. "Come on Gregory. You fly out here to tell me to dismantle a billion dollar federal law enforcement agency all on my own."

"Yes. The Director wants them emasculated. He doesn't want them threatening our survival. And you are to - in his words - kill every sonofabitch over there if that's what it takes."

"Why pay me? If he just wants them dead, why not just let the public kill them? That's probably what is going to start happening."

"That's precisely what we do not want to happen. If the population is angry and confused, we're fine. But if they're angry and confused and doing something about it, that's what we don't want, because once that starts going, we don't think we'll be able to stop it. Once they find out they can shoot the ATF, they can shoot the rest of us too," Naratova said.

"I don't share your concern about this. In fact, I kind of like what this shooter is stirring up. But since you are hell bent on paying us, Nick and I will do what we can. First, we'll see if we can locate the shooter, and after that, we'll work on finding some way to make ATF see the error of its ways."

"I have taken the liberty of depositing a large sum of money in your Cayman Islands account."

"I'm going to need a free hand to do this my way," Sam said.

"That's not a problem, within reason, of course,"

"There is very little reasonable about what you are asking me to do."

"That's a common occurrence in this business."

"The last time I worked for you, I ended up killing some of your people. I gather that pissed agency types off. I haven't worked for you since then."

"That's all behind us."

"There won't be interference from Ferriter?"

"The director and I are in control of this. Ferriter is out of the loop."

"All right then, Nick and I are going to need a direct line to computer research and priority access twenty-four hours a day."

"You'll have it. I'll call you with the number."

"Another thing. In the past, we've always been on our own. If we got caught, you never heard of us. Now I would like your assurances that if we get in difficulty with the locals, you will bail us out."

"You won't do us any good in jail. Just call. We'll get you out."

13

Sam and Nick spent the next ten days studying police reports from nine different agencies: the BATF, the Pittsburgh Police, the FBI, the Secret Service, the Internal Revenue Service, the Postal Police, Homeland Security, The Treasury Department, and the National Security Agency. They also visited and examined the sites of both shootings.

"How do you suppose the shooter got close enough to Kaplan to put the gun right up to his chest?" Nick said. "Normal training would have taught Kaplan to keep the shooter at arm's length until he could figure out a move."

"I know. It's an odd scenario," Sam said. "And there are no bruises on Kaplan to suggest either a struggle, or that he took some blows, or that he delivered any blows."

"Maybe the guy just walked past him and shoved the gun in his chest," Nick said.

"Let's try it." Sam said.

Sam put his plastic training gun in his belt and walked toward Nick, passing close enough to put the gun against his chest.

"Look how close I had to come to you to do that," Sam said.

"Yeah," Nick answered. "Kaplan wouldn't have let anybody get that close. Especially in a parking garage, where there's no reason to walk that near to somebody."

"What about the other shooting," Sam said. "Any ideas?"

"Yeah. I agree with the feds that the shooter had to be in some sort of vehicle. The bullet trajectory puts the shooter at street level, not in a building, and the only way he could be on the street and not in plain sight would be inside a vehicle."

"Okay. What kind?"

"Could be a copycat of that guy in D.C. who shot from a hide in the trunk of a car, sticking the rifle out a special cut where the license plate was hinged."

"Could be, but my gut tells me no. Too many differences in the situation. Big thing is that this guy uses different attacks, some close, some distant, but the D.C. guy always shot from the car," Sam said.

"I agree. That leaves us with an SUV or a van," Nick said.

"I don't think it was an SUV," Sam said. The only likely setup there would be to use one where the rear window rolled down or lifted up out of the way."

"Why wouldn't that be good?" Nick said.

"It would be workable, but the rear windows are huge. It would be easy to see in. I think this shooter was well hidden," Sam said. "Nobody saw anything."

"Sounds like a trained sniper," Nick said.

"Well, think about it, Nick. He was a sniper. It may have been close range, but this shooting was a sniper operation."

"So what did he use?" Nick said.

"I think it was a van," Sam said. "I think he did something to one of the rear windows of a two-door van. He somehow got the glass out of the way."

"Why are you so sure?"

"I'm not. It's just that it makes more sense than anything else, and our shooter is no dummy. If he uses a van, he won't be seen and the modification to that rear window is a relatively easy thing to do. Not only that, but a van would give him more room to rig up a sturdy and comfortable shooting position."

Sam and Nick put in a request to the CIA research department for a list of all body shops, especially those specializing in trucks, within a thirty-mile radius of Pittsburgh.

When the list came back four hours later, it had two thousand entries. Sam and Nick spent the next day going through the list, making calls, and categorizing body shops into those more and less likely to have made the modification to the van.

As Nick was working, Sam went to the phone and called Gregory Naratova.

"Gregory, we're going through a list of two thousand body shops," Sam said.

"I know," Naratova said. "I've already heard - at some length - from the computer people."

"Well, then. You're really gonna like this request."

"I can't wait."

"I want you to pinpoint each of these body shops on a map and match up those locations with satellite photos for four weeks before the second shooting," Sam said.

"What am I looking for?"

"You're looking for a van, any van, parked at or near any of the locations on the list."

"Jesus."

"I didn't ask for this job, Gregory."

"I'll get back to you."

Three days later, a list of six hundred ninety body shops came back. Sam was on the phone again. "Good work, Gregory."

"We've just used the overtime budget for the next five years."

"Here's an easy one for you. Now I need all of these body shops listed by gross income, highest to lowest," Sam said.

"That shouldn't be too hard," Naratova said.

By the end of the day, Sam had the list in order of decreasing income. Fourteen of the shops had filed no income tax forms for several years.

"My theory," Sam said, is that this guy wants to stay under the radar. If he used a body shop to modify his truck, it would be a small operation. Something like the shooter himself-under the radar."

"Where do we start?" Nick said.

"Let's start close in to Pittsburgh and then go outward," Sam said.

Within a week, they had located the body shop near Aaron 's house where the work to the van had been done. The owner of the shop was friendly and helpful after Sam and Nick showed him their fake Homeland Security badges.

"Yeah, I says to him - the old man-I says, what in the hell do you want this for? Just turn the a.c. on, I says, if you want some cool air. This is gonna cost you some money. I tell him that."

"Do you have the invoice for this job?" Nick said.

After ten minutes of searching, the owner turned it up. "Here it is," the body man said, handing over a sheet of paper.

"Aaron Silverman, it says. Do you know him?"

"Yeah. He don't live far from here. A nice old man. Known him for years. What's this about, anyway?"

"We're not at liberty to comment on an ongoing investigation," Sam said.

"So this modification," Nick said, "it allows him to lower one of the back-door windows, is that right?"

"Yeah. I had to jerry-rig a lot of it. Never done anything like that before.

You know. The window has to snap into the door tight, but you got to be able to pull it out from inside and lower it down."

"How'd you do it?" Nick said.

"Well, I took the window out and made a metal frame lined in rubber that holds the glass. I screwed the frame into the door and the back part of the frame snaps off, sort of like Reynolds windows. And then the glass is free and it slides down a track. When you want to close it, you slide the glass up the track and snap the rear part of the frame in again."

Nick and Sam drove three miles to Aaron Silverman's house, where they found the van parked on the street. It was late afternoon, and they decided to have something to eat while they waited for darkness. After dinner, Nick changed into a black jumpsuit and surgical gloves and picked the lock of the truck, going in through the back doors. The truck was empty. Once inside, Nick extracted five plastic bags with rags in each bag. He vigorously rubbed the ceiling with one rag, the floor with another, the two sides of the truck with rags from the third and fourth bags, and the insides of the doors with the fifth. He carefully labeled each plastic bag and returned the rags to their respective bags after he had used them to get a sample.

Sam drove the plastic bags to the airport, where they met an agent who took them directly to a CIA plane going to the central lab at Langley. The lab called forty minutes after receiving the samples. Samples from all five bags were positive for gunshot residue. Vihtavuori rifle powder. Likely a handload. Powder originates in Finland. Commonly used by expert riflemen. Traits are accuracy in medium weight bullets and low muzzle flash.

Sam and Nick were sipping their Glenlivit later that evening when the phone rang. Caller ID indicated it was Naratova. They didn't answer and Naratova said to the machine, "What the hell's going on, Sam?"

Sam took another sip and said, "You ever notice. . . . they always think they're in control."

"Ain't it the truth," Nick snorted.

14

For the next three days, Sam and Nick were parked down the block from the van when Aaron came out of his house around 8:00 o'clock, got in his van, and drove to the coffee shop on the South Side where he met Jamie and Jesse for breakfast. The first day, Aaron simply went home after eating with his companions.

The second day, however, Jamie and Aaron left in the van and Jesse followed them in a pick up truck. They took route 28 north to Millvale, exiting at Grant Avenue to Babcock Blvd, and then turning off Babcock at the dirt road which led to the Millvale Sportsmen's Club. Sam followed the van and the pickup truck down a winding dirt road to the club. The van and the truck parked at the rifle range and Sam and Nick drove on past, parking further away from the range. They watched as the three old men got their shooting gear out and set up on benches. They were shooting some sort of bolt gun, an M-1 Garand, and an M-1A. They stayed for two hours shooting targets at 100 and 200 yards.

"These guys gotta be eighty," Nick said.

"Yeah, but they can shoot," Sam said, as they watched Jesse and Jamie walk down to the 200 yard target to put up another target and check the one they had just shot.

A man came up to Sam and Nick to ask them if they were members. They said that they were not, but that they were thinking of joining and just wanted to look around. The man was friendly and told them to stay as long as they liked.

On the third day, Sam and Nick went to the customary breakfast place and approached the old men as they sat at their customary table. They had finished eating and were sitting, talking and drinking their coffee. They seemed to be in high spirits.

"Gentlemen," Sam said. "Do you mind if we join you?"

The old men glanced at one another. They had been coming here for years and no one had ever asked to join them.

"Sit down," Jamie Berenger said.

Sam and Nick pulled up two chairs.

"We haven't seen you here before," Aaron said.

"No. We're new. But I guess you guys have been coming here for a while?" Nick said.

"Oh, yeah," Jesse said. "We're old timers."

"You gotta watch the eggs," Jamie Berenger said. "They'll overcook them."

Sam laughed. "Well, we just wanted to introduce ourselves. I think we have some of the same interests."

"What's that?" Aaron said.

"We both like shooting and neither of us likes the government," Nick said.

The old men froze. "I don't follow you," Jamie Berenger said.

"We think you guys are the ones who have been shooting up the BATF," Sam said.

"We don't know nothing about that," Jesse said.

"Take it easy," Nick said. "We're not cops."

"And besides that," Sam said, "We're on your side."

"If you're not cops, who are you?" Jesse said.

"I'm Sam Budda and this is Nick Savarese," Sam said, smiling.

It took a minute for the names to register, and then Jamie Berenger blurted out, "What the hell? You work for us. You're Sam Budda?"

"Yep."

"And I'm Nick."

"Damn," Jesse said. "Damn. How'd you find us?"

"We swabbed residue samples out of your van, the one that was recently modified to allow you to lower the window from inside, and they tested positive for powder residue. What was it, Nick?"

"I think is was Vihtavuori N110," Nick said. "Kind of an unusual powder. One that might be used by an expert rifleman. This powder is especially known for its accuracy and low muzzle flash."

"You don't use Vihtavuori powder do you?" Sam said to Aaron .

"How did you know to look in the van?" Aaron said.

"Satellite photos showed your van at a body shop shortly before the shooting. We started checking out vans that showed up at body shops for modifications to their rear windows. Nobody but you had the windows altered so they could be removed and your van tested positive for powder," Sam said.

"Moreover, military records that we ran after we identified the van show that all of you were crack shots in the service. Way beyond "Marksman" level," Nick said.

"Satellite photos and military records?" Jesse said. "How the hell did you manage that?"

"It was quite a coincidence, really. You guys started shooting up the ATF and our old employers at the CIA contacted us to see who was doing it. They chose us because we live in Pittsburgh. We're hired by one government agency to find out who has been shooting up another government agency. So we had access to satellite photos and military records through the CIA. We're supposed to stop the killing, but we're also supposed to put the brakes on the BATF," Sam said

"What do you mean," Jamie Berenger said, "put the brakes on?"

"Make them stop acting like thugs and assholes is the best way I know to describe it," Sam said.

"That would be quite an accomplishment," Aaron ventured.

"Let's talk about you guys for a minute," Nick said. "We need to understand what you're doing and why."

"We're just . . . "

"Wait a minute, Jesse," Jamie said. "What will you do when you find out what we're doing?"

"We'll decide whether we can work with you or whether we have to work separately. You may have to lay low for a while, or even permanently," Sam said.

"So you're not going to arrest us?" Aaron said.

"Hell, no," Nick said. "As Sam said, we may want to work with you."

"How could you work with us?" Jesse said.

"We'll get to that later. Now tell us what you're trying to accomplish," Sam said.

"We're trying to get the government to let this guy Mulhaney go," Jamie said.

"And we want them to stop acting like Nazis. We want them to stop harassing people and threatening them with guns and midnight raids and interfering in their lives," Aaron said.

"And we want them to leave our guns alone," Jesse said.

There was quiet at the table.

Finally, Sam said, "We're on your side. We want the same things."

"We saw them on television in their black suits. We saw black suits just like them sixty years ago in Europe. We didn't give in to those black suits and we're not giving in to these," Aaron said.

"Easy," Sam said. "We know. We agree. We don't like 'em any better than you do."

"My family died in the Warsaw Ghetto," Aaron said. "We want people here to have guns, to have a chance against the thugs when they come."

"You three would take a few with you," Nick said.

"Damn right," Jamie Berenger said. "And we'd organize a resistance."

"What about modern weapons?" Sam said.

"We're not dumb, Sam," Jesse said. "We know we're outgunned, but a man with a .30-06 can still kill thugs, and in order to kill the man with the .30-06, the government has to come out in the open, surround his house with two hundred men, and show everybody how they're killing people. That's where they'll have trouble, because that will spark more resistance."

"The Germans all said they didn't know what the government was doing to the Jews, and many Jews didn't know where they were being taken. But with today's communication, that couldn't ever be claimed in our time," Aaron said. "If the government starts killing people, everyone all over the world will know about it within minutes."

"The importance of guns isn't that they would allow anyone to prevail against the army, but that pockets of armed resistance would force the government to be so oppressive that the population as a whole would be outraged and resist," Jesse said.

"On the other hand," Sam said, "if the public gets used to seeing the government attack people, there would be no resistance to any act of oppression, since oppression would have become the norm. The public would be used to it. Is that it?"

"That's right, and that's why we are concerned about the Mulhaney case," Jesse said. "If you think the Mulhaney case is okay, almost anything they do after that will probably be okay too."

"You got to remember, we're not alone in this," Jamie Berenger said. "We estimate there are at least a million people out there just like us."

"That's good to hear," Nick said, "but there's really no way to be sure of that."

"We have a way," Jesse said. "You just got to us a little too soon."

"What's your way?" Sam said.

"If BATF doesn't back off pretty soon, we plan to put the names of every BATF agent in the country on the internet, with the suggestion that people who oppose this horseshit start shooting agents. We'd include their addresses, social security numbers, and their pictures," Aaron said.

"How could you get this information?" Nick asked.

"I hacked into a computer that serves as their payroll organizer years ago," Aaron said, "and we've updated the list every month since we first got in."

"If agents start dropping like flies," Jesse said, "we'll know there are a lot of us. If nothing happens, we'll know we're in this alone."

15

Sam and Nick spent the next two days with the old men, learning who they were, what their capabilities were, what they could be trusted to do well, and how practical it would be to enlist their aid in the Herculean task of curbing the BATF.

On the third day, Aaron said, "We've decided we can trust you. We're going to show you our secret weapon. Tell them, Jamie."

"Some years ago, I built a special rifle. I worked with a guy named Hans Braun off in some little town in Ohio. He's into all kinds of unusual and powerful rifle builds. This rifle seems like it might have some application for the present situation."

"Sounds interesting," Sam said. "Is this the kind of rifle that would draw attention if you shot it at the gun club?"

"I think so," Jamie Berenger laughed. "It makes quite a noise."

"Why don't you guys follow us out to our test range," Nick said. "It's out past Monroeville on Route 22. We have 200 acres that are pretty secluded and we can shoot 400 yards into a big cliff."

"Sounds perfect," Aaron said.

An hour and a half later, Sam's Land Cruiser and Aaron's van turned onto a dirt road leading through woods to a cleared area about forty yards wide and almost 500 yards long, ending in a high shale cliff. Two sturdy shooting benches were placed at the near end of the range.

"Boy, is this perfect," Jesse said.

Sam said, "Let's see what you got."

Jamie Berenger and Jesse each took one end of a special case that was longer and heavier than a normal rifle case and carried it to one of the shooting benches. Jamie Berenger released the four heavy latches and opened the case.

Inside was one of the largest-caliber rifles Sam had ever seen. It dwarfed a .50 BMG bolt gun.

"What is this?" Sam said.

" It's a .950 JDJ," Jamie Berenger said, proudly. "Here's the round it shoots."

"Jesus," Nick said.

Sam went to the Landcruiser and returned with a small tool kit containing, among other things, a pair of calipers. The round measured 4.845 inches in length. The web area of the case measured 1.161inches. From the base of the casing to its mouth was 2.885 inches. The bullet itself measured .9495 inches diameter at the ogive. A 95 caliber bullet!

"This looks like a 20mm cannon casing," Nick said.

"Normally, I would use a 20mm casing necked down for this bullet, but since 20mm's haven't been available for some time, I have a friend who mills these for me out of a solid bar of brass."

"What about this bullet? It's massive," Sam said.

"It's 3500 grains," Jamie said, smiling. "Solid brass. He mills the bullets too."

"Jesus," Sam said. " 3500 grains is half a pound. "

Nick said, "A fifty caliber Browning machine gun bullet weighs 750 grains. It would take almost five BMG bullets to equal this oned."

"Yep," Aaron said. "It's a pretty interesting bullet."

"What kind of recoil do you get with this round?" Nick said. "I see you have a huge muzzle brake on the end of the barrel."

"Well, you don't want to shoot too many of these, but the rifle weighs seventy pounds, so that helps a lot," Jamie said.

"Obviously, this isn't a factory round," Sam said. "What's the load? "

"Two hundred grains of Hodgdon's 870 powder," Jamie Berenger answered, with a wide grin. "I had these cases swaged to accept a .50-caliber machine gun primer."

"Muzzle velocity?" Nick asked.

"I haven't chronographed it for years," Jamie Berenger said, "but when I did, it was about 2800 feet per second. But that might have been the 2700 grain bullet. I can't remember."

Jamie placed the rifle on one of the shooting benches, resting on its built-in bipod. He mounted the quick-detachable scope onto the huge rifle.

"This is a Zeiss 6.5 x 20 x with a 50mm objective and a Mil Dot reticle," Jamie said.

"What's the field of view at 400 yards?" Sam asked.

"It's about five or six feet at 100 yards, so about 20 to 25 feet at 400 yards,"

Jamie Berenger said. "I'm sure you can shoot this gun out to fifteen hundred yards or so, but I've never had a scope that would let me do that," Jamie Berenger said.

Nick took a target out to the 400-yard target stand. The target consisted of a white circle about the size of a garbage can lid with a black circle inside the size of a man's head. When the range was clear, Jamie Berenger settled down on the bench with the big rifle. The fore-end was supported on the integral bipod. The stock, tight against Jamie's shoulder, also rested on a large sandbag on the bench just behind the trigger housing.

Everyone put on protective shooters' earmuffs, and Sam watched the target through a Leica 45 X spotting scope mounted on the second bench. When the round went off, there was a jarring concussion and a trememdous ball of fire blossomed around the muzzle brake.

Dust and debris filled the air around the target, as the bullet pulverized twenty pounds of cliff rock into dust.

When Sam recovered from the surprise of the concussion, he steadied the spotting scope and focused on the target.

"You're in the black at 6:00 o'clock," he said.

The round had hit the target low in the black area. It would have hit a human target low in the head. Jamie Berenger smiled and worked the massive bolt, which flung the empty casing free of the smoking chamber.

"Let's try a penetration test for this big boy," Sam said. "We keep some materials here for just such occasions as this one. Give us a few minutes to set something up,"

There was a stack of concrete blocks and steel plates out at 300 yards. Sam and Nick drove out to the blocks and began to load them into the Land Cruiser. They drove twenty-seven blocks to the 400-yard marker and began to build a cube of three rows of blocks, three blocks wide and three blocks high. Between each row there was a distance of six inches, and in the areas behind the first and second rows, Sam placed two hardened steel plates about one-half inch thick, each weighing about 150 pounds.

"That should do it," Nick said.

"Nope," Sam said. "We need to fill up the holes in these concrete blocks with dirt."

"You're kidding," Nick said.

"Trust me," Sam smiled.

It took them twenty minutes to fill the blocks and the spaces between them with sand and gravel. When they finally got back to the shooting benches, Jamie Berenger was ready. Sam and Nick had a long drink of water and then put on their ear muffs. Sam directed Jamie to shoot for the middle of the block wall which would center the shot on the steel plates.

Once again there was a huge concussion when the rifle went off, followed closely by a deafening blast, but this time the noise and concussion were accompanied by a spectacular sight at 400 yards. The blocks literally exploded. Fragments shot sixty feet into the air and a huge cloud of debris formed over where the wall of blocks had been.

When the dust cleared, everyone walked out to the target. The first two rows of concrete blocks had been obliterated. Some of the blocks in the third row were scattered over an area twenty yards behind their original location, and some had simply been exploded into dust. Both hardened steel plates had been penetrated with a clean ninety-five caliber hole and were thrown behind their original location, one fifteen yards behind and the other twenty-seven yards back and to the side. The sand and gravel that had been shoveled into the concrete blocks was dusted over the entire field behind the target.

"What did you say you wanted to do with this gun?" Sam said to Jamie Berenger.

16

"This is Sam Budda. I talked to your predecessor about the shooting of ATF agents."

"I know who you are, Mr. Budda. What can I do for you?" Dale Ferrara said. Ferrara was the new head of office of the Pittsburgh BATF, the successor of Corky James, who had been the head of the BATF office when Sam was first interviewed, but who now was dead.

"I have received another message from my client," Sam said.

"Come in and we'll talk about it."

"No. You're welcome to come here or we can talk on the phone, but I'm not coming there. The last time I did, I ended up in jail."

"You'll end up in jail again if you aren't here in half an hour," Ferrara said.

The phone went dead and Sam hung up. Since the BATF did not want to talk, Sam decided to go to the gym for a workout and then to a late breakfast near Bloomfield.

When Sam came out of Ritter's Diner on Baum Boulevard, he was surrounded by eight plainclothes ATF agents with guns drawn and pointed at Sam's chest. Three black Ford Crown Victorias blocked traffic on Baum Boulevard for as far as one could see.

Sam raised his hands while two agents shoved pistols in his ribs, and threw him against the building. One ripped the Les Baer .45 from Sam's hip holster and the other fastened Sam's hands behind his back with wire ties. They led him to one of the black Fords and pushed him into the back seat, banging his head against the roof ledge.

The wire ties were cutting off circulation, and Sam asked for them to be loosened, but he was ignored. The driver sped recklessly through traffic on his way to the federal building downtown, weaving in and out of lanes on Bigelow

Boulevard, and scraped the frame of the car entering the basement. All eight agents crowded into the elevator with Sam and they seemed intent on crushing him with their collective weight. They got off at the sixth floor and trooped into the ATF office, past the secure waiting room, down a corridor. The agent who had tightened the wire ties yanked Sam along by his necktie. By the time the group stopped in front of a large desk manned by the executive assistant to the Chief Agent, Sam's hands had lost all feeling. The agent pulling Sam said something to the executive assistant and the door to the Chief Agent's office buzzed. The agent opened the door and pulled Sam inside.

The corner office overlooked Liberty Avenue with the Allegheny River beynd. Dale Ferrara sat smug behind his desk. An agent shifted Sam forward. Ferrara hooked his thumbs in his suspenders and looked at Sam. His threadbard shirt was too tight and his pasty jowls squeezed over the collar. An American flag sat to Ferrara's right, reminding those in attendance that this was the Federal Government.

"Well, hotshot, I guess you'll think twice before you fuck with me again," he said.

"I've got a number for you," Sam said.

"Say what, hotshot?"

"Call 600-472-3373."

Ferrara recognized the 600 number as one employed by undercover federal agents for verification of their identity.

"Say again," Ferrara said.

Sam repeated the number.

Within two minutes, Gregory Naratova was on the phone.

"Naratova," he said.

"This is Chief Agent Ferrara, Pittsburgh ATF," Ferrara said.

"I see that by the caller i.d.," Naratova said. "What do you need?"

"I have a man in custody who gave me this number."

"Sam Budda, I would guess."

"Yes. Whom am I speaking to?"

"Gregory Naratova, Deputy Director, Central Intelligence."

"Is this guy one of yours, Mr. Naratova?"

"Mr. Budda is engaged in a covert operation reporting only to the Director and the President. Does that tell you what you need to know?"

"Yes, sir. Can you give me that in writing?"

"What I'll give you in writing, Mr. Ferrara, is your immediate termination notice if you impede Mr. Budda in any way."

"Ahhhh. Yes, sir."

"Keep Naratova on the phone," Sam said. "And have this goon cut my hands free."

Ferrara nodded to the agent who had tightened the wire ties on Sam's wrists. The agent didn't like being called a goon and jerked Sam's wrists uncomfortably upward as he cut him loose.

Sam's hands were beginning to turn gray and he rubbed them to restore circulation. Ferrara held the phone out, but Sam shook his head and continued rubbing his wrists, leaving Ferrara's holding the phone in mid-air.

"I can't feel my hands," Sam said, continuing to rub his wrists, "you'll have to wait a minute."

Ferrara said into the phone, "He wants to talk to you but he can't hold the phone yet. Give him a minute."

"Don't tell me one of your people wired him up that tight," Naratova said.

"Yeah. Well, we didn't know he was one of us," Ferrara said. "His hands seem to be getting some color back now."

Sam kept rubbing his hands vigorously. Ferrara waited nervously. His desktop was empty except for an eight-by-ten photograph in a heavy wooden frame of Ferrara's wife and kids. Ferrara rubbed the edge of the frame with one hand while he held the phone in the other.

Sam reached as if to take the receiver, but in a move that was too fast to be intercepted, he seized the framed photograph. With the photograph in his right hand, he pivoted on his left foot, and slammed the edge of the photograph into the face of the agent standing behind him. The agent flew backward and skidded across the floor on his back, with bone showing through the skin on his forehead where the frame had impacted. Blood gushed from the wound. The momentum of the blow carried Sam off his feet, and he sprawled on the floor next to the agent. Two agents grabbed Sam, picked him up and slammed him against a bookcase, jarring its contents and then the bookcase itself onto the floor.

"Enough," Ferrara roared, putting the phone down on his desk.

The agents released Sam, who adjusted his torn shirt and walked over to Ferrara's desk. He picked up the phone and said, "This is Sam. We had a little disagreement here. Tell the head goon I'm going to walk out of here and that I'll see him in my office in the morning. And tell him to have one of the other goons give me back my gun."

Sam handed the phone to Ferrara. Ferrara's face flushed beet red as he put the phone to his ear. He nodded to the agent behind Sam, who returned the Les Baer with the slide locked open and no magazine.

Sam looked impassively at the agent, released the slide, and holstered the weapon. He turned and walked out the door.

* * *

When Sam and Nick arrived at their office the next morning, Dale Ferrara and three ATF agents stood outside the door.

"Morning," Sam said, opening the door.

Ferrara said nothing. He and his agents followed Sam into the office. Nick brought up the rear.

"You wanted to see me?" Sam said.

"You damned well know I want to see you," Ferrara said.

"Ask your men to wait outside," Sam said.

Nick smiled. The agents were still boiling from yesterday.

"They're with me," Ferrara said.

"Okay. You can all wait outside. When you decide to leave them in the car, you can come in yourself. Until then, all of you outside."

"Wait in the car," Ferrara said, visibly angry.

The agents filed out.

"Have a chair," Sam said, moving around to the swivel chair behind his desk. Nick sat in an armchair alongside Ferrara.

"What's he doing here?" Ferrara said.

"This will be hard for you," Sam said, "but you don't determine who sits in this room. I do. You are used to pushing your weight around and telling people what to do, but that doesn't work here. "

"You're out of line," Ferrara said, "and if that goddam spook hadn't taken you under his wing, I'd fry you up for dinner."

"I'm sure you would. In fact, that's why we're here. You BATF types have been frying people for some time and there are a few people who don't like it. In fact, they're apparently thinking of frying you up for dinner," Sam said.

"I'll never forget what you did to my agent," Ferrara said.

"And I'll never forget what your agents, including that goon with the smashed-in face, did to me when they brought me into your office," Sam said.

"Why did you call me?" Ferrara shot back.

"My client is impatient with your response to his demand that you let Mulhaney go, and he is going to start shooting again if you don't get it done."

"The Director says we will let Mulhaney go, but only if your client meets with me face to face and makes the request," Ferrara said.

"Why would he do that?" Sam said.

"We'll grant him immunity for the two murders he has committed already, but we want to know who he is so we can keep him from starting this all over again next year," Ferrara said.

"What assurance does he have that you will do what you say?" Sam said.

"That's what you're for. You know what we're offering, and if we don't do it, you can squeal on us."

"That's if you don't shoot me first," Sam said.

"That would be illegal," Ferrara smiled.

"Yeah, it would," Sam said.

There was a pause in the conversation. Ferrara wanted is threat to soak in. He was feeling smug. Budda might have the spooks on is side, but he was no match for a Federal Agency.

"You need to give me your attention for a minute Mr. Ferrara," Nick said, "You're a dumb prick so I'm going to explain this slowly. You spend a lot of time behind a desk and you hear a lot of shit about the majesty of the Federal government. You even begin to believe it. But here's what things boil down to. If you fuck with Sam, I will kill you."

Ferrara blanched.

"Not only that," Nick continued, "I'll have your entire family killed, and anyone who even thinks of you as a friend. People are already in place to do it."

Ferrara squirmed. He was used to being part of an army of police. He relied on sheer numbers to overwhelm any opposition. But now he had only himself. Ferrara realized he was breathing in rapid shallow gulps. These guys were crazy.

"It's not good to make threats," Ferrara mumbled.

"We don't make threats, Ferrara. We explain to people how not to get themselves killed," Nick said, pulling out a small notebook and turning the pages. "You wife's name is Pamela and she works downtown at Macy's. You have two children, aged six and eight, who attend Sacred Heart School in Shadyside. Your mother's name is Mary, and she lives alone in Shaler. Your father is dead. You have a brother in Denver, Wilson, and he also has a family. I have assets in place to kill all of these people. Sam dies, they die."

"All right. I get it," Ferrara said. Ferrara was now standing. He couldn't wait to leave. He suddenly felt hot and nauseous. He had to get out of there. He was beginning to sweat profusely.

"Where and when do you want to meet?" Sam said.

"It's up to you and to him. Just let me know. I'll be there."

"I'm just the messenger," Sam said. "I have no idea whether this guy if my guy will want to do this, but I'll give him your message."

Ferrara left the office without another word. Sam and Nick looked at each other.

"I think he was getting a little overheated," Sam said. "Did you notice that?"

17

"I'll do it," Aaron said. "Let's get it going."

"Wait a minute, Aaron. This is almost certainly a set-up. They're not going to give you immunity for killing two of their own," Sam said.

"I know that," Aaron said.

"Then why do it?"

"Because it forces them to show what they really are," Aaron said.

"I don't think so. The public will just see the guy who shot two ATF agents got arrested. The ATF will be heroes," Sam said.

"He's right," Jesse said. "Those bastards won't give you immunity. They're going to arrest you for murder."

The conversation continued for three hours, and at the end of it, Aaron was still adamant. He would meet with the ATF man.

"In that case," Sam said, "we have to clean your house. Every gun and all gun materials have to be removed. Any books that might be interpreted as subversive have to go. The van has to be restored to its original state, and the whole inside of the van has to be scrubbed. All of your clothes need to be cleaned to remove powder residue. The entire inside of the house needs to be scrubbed and vacuumed and the carpets need to be shampooed."

"Jesus," Aaron said. "All that?"

"Yes. They will use every little thing against you. We're going to remove from your house any trace of your association with firearms. Don't misunderstand, there is nothing wrong with firearms, but district attorneys are known for twisting the fact that one owns a gun, or handloaded ammunition, or reads books about gun-related things into the theory that he is obviously a mass murderer. So we try to cut that off. Understand?"

"Yes."

"Then let's get started," Sam said.

The old men dismantled Aaron's reloading room and over the next several days carted his components, reloading equipment, and guns to Jamie Berenger' house, ten miles away. They even unbolted Aaron's workbenches from the wall and disposed of the lumber in a dump. Nick arranged for the house to be scrubbed by a janitorial service and supervised the work. When they finished scrubbing the floors and walls, they power-washed the basement with a powerful soap. Sam helped Aaron go through all his personal records and books. Most of his personal papers were destroyed in an industrial shredder rented for the occasion, and twelve cartons of books were dropped off at various Salvation Army sites or given to Jamie Berenger and Jesse. Every piece of Aaron's clothing was sent to the dry cleaner's or to an industrial laundry service. Another specialized service cleaned every upholstered chair or couch in the house. The bed linen was boiled in special washers. The hard disc from Aaron's computer was sent to the CIA to be wiped clean, and the computer was placed in a thrift store donation drop. All of Aaron's assets were assigned to his attorney for safekeeping.

Ten days after they had begun, they were done. Aaron's life was as sterile as it would ever be. All that remained was a bare house that had been scrubbed clean. There wasn't even a pad to write on.

New life seemed to have been pumped into the old men. They moved around almost jauntily and talked animatedly about what they were doing. Aaron was excited and ready for anything.

* * *

Sam drove Aaron to downtown Pittsburgh the day after the house had been sterilized. The meeting had been arranged for 10:00 a.m. in the middle of the PPG Plaza. The plaza was a stone courtyard about sixty yards square surrounded by tall glass buildings. If Ferrara was not there when they arrived, they were to take a seat at one of the outdoor tables on the plaza and have a drink while they waited.

On the way downtown, Sam said, "You know, Aaron, this isn't going to work. They are not going to let you go. They are going to arrest you and charge you with murder."

"I know," the old man said.

"Are you sure you want to do this?"

"I'm sure."

"They're not exactly gentle. I've seen them operate."

"So have I."

"They won't care if they hurt you. They're gonna beat you up. They're hungry to get even for the men you've killed."

"I know that."

"There's nothing I can say, is there?"

"No."

Sam parked the Land Cruiser at a lot near the corner of Stanwix Street and the Boulevard of the Allies. He didn't want to drive too close to the plaza. He didn't want to risk having ATF impound the vehicle. They would walk two blocks to the plaza.

The plaza was almost as big as a football field, surrounded on all sides by the towering PPG buildings, and paved with giant flagstones with a tall sculpture in the middle. It was empty except for a few people walking with their coffee on the way to work. There was no sign of Ferrara.

They walked to the middle of the plaza, but still there was no sign of Ferrara.

Sam knew that foot traffic on the plaza was usually brisk at this time of the morning, and that was his first indication that something was different.

"You want to sit down?" Sam said.

Before Aaron could to answer, two hundred men in black battle dress, helmets and flack vests emerged from the buildings that surrounded the plaza with rifles shouldered and began to advance on all sides at a fast shuffle-walk.

"Don't move," Sam said quietly.

"I couldn't if I wanted to," the old man said, plainly terrified.

"Raise your hands," Sam said.

Sam and Aaron stood in the center of the plaza with their hands held high as the two hundred federal agents advanced toward them in a circle. The circle closed on Sam and the old man and some agents had to drop back into a second, then a third, then a fourth row.

When the helmeted assault troops closed within five yards, one of the troopers commanded, "on your face, scummies. On your fuckin face."

Sam took the old man's elbow and was easing him down when a trooper hit Sam in the middle of his back with a rifle butt, knocking him sprawling onto the flagstones. Another trooper butt-stroked the old man, who collapsed in a heap, unconscious.

Sam tried to get to the old man, but he was kicked in the head, the back, the arms, and the legs by every trooper who could reach him. He too was knocked unconscious. Both men were bound tightly with wire ties, hands and feet, rolled onto stretchers, and shoved into waiting trucks. When Sam and

Aaron came to, they were shackled to beds in the federal building.

"How you doin?" Sam said, turning his head toward Aaron.

"I been better," Aaron said.

"Ferrara must have decided he didn't need to talk to you after all," Sam said.

"Looks that way."

The door opened and Ferrara strutted in, thumbs hooked onto his suspenders. He smiled at Sam and then Aaron . "So. . . . It's the tough guy and the old man. Cop killers. . . ."

"Wait a minute Mr. BATF," Aaron said. "I'm the cop killer. Sam is just the guy who carries messages."

"Sure, sure, sure," Ferrara said.

"I suppose you think my lawyer kills cops too," Aaron said.

"Wouldn't be surprised," Ferrara said.

"What happened to immunity?" Sam said.

"I lied."

"You know, I don't work alone," Aaron said.

"Give me the names of your buddies and we'll bring them in to see you," Ferrara said.

"I think he's trying to tell you, Ferrara, that when the guys he works with find out you arrested him, they will be unhappy," Sam said.

At that moment, Bradford Hayes walked in with a writ of habeas corpus.

"Let him go, Mr. Ferrara," Hayes said.

Ferrara looked at the writ and nodded to one of the agents who had accompanied him in the room. The agent released Sam's shackles and Sam slowly sat up.

"You might want to think twice before you mess with the BATF again, Mr. Budda," Ferrara said.

"You are a truly stupid man," Sam said.

Hayes whispered a few words to Aaron , then helped Sam walk out of the room. He took Sam directly to the emergency room of Shadyside Hospital, where he knew the director of emergency services, and Sam was treated for a concussion, bone bruises, bruised ribs, and deep cuts.

18

Sam and Nick watched from two blocks away as ATF agents swarmed over Aaron's house. There were twenty agents and assorted trucks and cars, some marked, some unmarked, parked in Aaron's yard and on the street around his house. The neighbors stood on their porches or peered stealthily through drawn blinds at the ATF agents as they came and went. There was a steady line of agents going into the house with sledgehammers and sawzalls. Another line of agents came out of the house carrying plastic garbage bags. Two agents struggled with what appeared to be a section of a wall, which they loaded into a truck. Still other agents had rolls of carpet. By mid-afternoon, ATF was gone and the house was sealed with yellow tape, which said "Crime Scene Do Not Enter."

That afternoon, Sam called Ferrara.

"Haven't you had enough, smart guy," Ferrara said.

"I got a communication from another person who claims to be a member of Aaron's group. This guy says that if you don't release Aaron and discontinue the prosecution against Mulhaney, you will lose some more agents."

"You tell your buddy that we're gonna prosecute Aaron for murder and tell him we'll get him too, just like we got Aaron."

"I'll tell him," Sam said. "Any other message?"

"Just a message to you hotshot. I ain't through with you yet. You just keep that in mind. You and all your gun nut buddies are gonna end up in the same place."

Sam hung up. Nick sipped his coffee. "I don't think he likes me," Sam said. Nick smiled.

For the next three days, the headlines were full of the arrest of the ATF killer, an eighty-one year old World War II veteran. The killer's attorney,

Bradford Hayes, gave brief interviews in which he said that his client was a patriot and that he had appeared voluntarily to meet with the BATF pursuant to a promise of immunity for any participation in the killing of the two ATF agents. He said that ATF had reneged on its promise and that whatever his client had done, it was a patriotic act in response to the excesses of the BATF.

Talk shows buzzed with endless discussions of why an eighty-one-year-old man would do such a thing and editorials condemned vigilante justice. Police organizations condemned the killing of their brother officers, and the United States Attorney for the Western District of Pennsylvania promised swift and sure justice. The Director of ATF appeared before Congress and praised the outstanding work of ATF agents in accomplishing the almost impossible task of finding the man responsible for the killing of ATF agents. "Only the most highly dedicated, professional, capable agents could have possibly have solved these terrible crimes," he said.

The Director of ATF also announced that he would go to Pittsburgh to personally decorate the agents of that office with citations for bravery and outstanding service to the United States. "Thank God we have come to the end of this chapter of senseless violence," he said on Prime Time Television. "Now it is time to recognize the brave men and women who, on a daily basis, risk their lives so that you all can live in safety, and who solved this crime against heavy odds. It is a great day for federal law enforcement."

* * *

Pittsburgh International Airport is located eighteen miles north and west of the city. The main route connecting the airport and the city is the parkway, also known as Route 376. Near the city, the parkway goes through a tunnel, which opens onto the Fort Pitt Bridge and a spectacular view of downtown Pittsburgh. At that point, one is roughly a mile from the federal building in downtown Pittsburgh, home of the BATF regional offices.

Between the airport and the tunnel, the parkway winds through valleys, industrial areas, and semi populated neighborhoods nestled in trees and hills. Two miles from the tunnel, the parkway passes under a tall railroad trestle made of heavy timbers and steel braces. The tracks are one hundred fifty feet above the road and they disappear into woods high overhead on either side of the road.

Sam and Jamie Berenger sat by the side of the tracks in the hills near the parkway. The sound of cars and trucks passing far below was almost mesmerizing, steady and undulating like waves. The heavy rifle rested, muzzle up, on a rolled-up mat near where the two men sat, sipping coffee from a thermos.

"You know," Sam said, "when we get out there on that trestle, if a train comes, we're done."

'I know it," Jamie Berenger said. "Mincemeat."

"You see the shot," Sam said. "It looks to me like about two hundred fifty yards."

"Yeah," Jamie Berenger said. "Two problems. I'm shooting down and the car will be moving toward me."

"Probably about sixty miles an hour, maybe faster. We'll get Nick to follow them and call in their speed."

"I'm gonna guess that when he gets to that middle pillar on the bridge, I should be holding on the road in front of the bumper," Jamie Berenger said.

"Sounds right," Sam said. "A hit in the engine compartment is really what we want. But even if you overshoot, the round will penetrate the passenger compartment and cause all kinds of damage. So either one will be o.k."

Sam's cell phone rang. Nick and Jesse were sitting alongside Route 60 near the airport, waiting for the appearance of the convoy of black cars transporting the director of ATF from the airport to the downtown office of BATF. The director was as good as his word: he was going to present medals to the Pittsburgh ATF staff. The convoy passed Nick at 2:07 p.m. Two motorcycle policemen led a black Suburban followed by an armored Lincoln Town Car, another Suburban, and two more motorcycle policemen.

"They're just leaving," Nick said.

"Got it," Sam answered. "Can you give us an estimate of road speed?"

"Wait a minute. I'll call you back," Nick said.

Nick accelerated the Audi A8 and caught up with the convoy. They were passing everything on the road with lights and sirens blazing. Nick tracked them for a mile or so and then called Sam. "They're going about 70," he said. "I think the motorcycles are slowing them down."

"Got it," Sam said.

"They're going about 70," Sam said to Jamie Berenger. "Let's get ready."

Sam slung the seventy-pound rifle and tucked the rolled-up sleeping mat under one arm, then headed for the tracks. Jamie Berenger followed with a large knapsack containing sandbags, the coffee, and five of the 3500-grain rounds for the rifle. Sam stepped on the railroad ties that made up the bridge and began walking on the ties toward the center of the trestle bridge. The road below was clearly visible between the ties. There were no safety railings on the trestle. It was made for trains, not people. Sam continued down the tracks onto the trestle with Jamie Berenger behind him.

When Sam got to roughly the middle of the bridge, he stopped and signaled for Jamie Berenger to unload the sandbags. Traffic zipped by below. Jamie

Berenger put three large sandbags down, one on the rails and two on a railroad tie. Sam rolled the mat out on the railroad ties as Jamie Berenger backed up to allow the mat to unroll. When it was flat, Jamie Berenger knelt down and Sam placed the fore-end of the heavy rifle on the sandbagged rail. Jamie Berenger slid down into a sideways prone position and fixed two of the sandbags under his right armpit and under the stock. He removed the scope covers and dialed the scope down to 6.5 X. Sam checked the scope for tightness and Jamie Berenger settled in to a shooting position.

Sam handed Jamie Berenger a 3500-grain round and the shooter chambered it in the big rifle, thunking the oversized bolt closed and again sighting through the scope with both eyes open. The rifle was pointed at the road where the car would be at a distance of two-to-three hundred yards.

Sam handed Jamie Berenger a pair of electronic earmuffs and he put on his own. These muffs would allow the two men to communicate but would shield them from the terrific blast of the rifle by electronically shutting down their sound transmitting circuits at the moment the rifle was fired.

"Are you steady?" Sam asked.

"Steady. Stand by with the reload," Jamie Berenger said.

"It's ready," Sam said. "I'll alert you when I see the motorcycles top the ridge."

Jamie Berenger lay silent and steady, his one foot braced against the rails to his back, his shoulder firmly and comfortably on one sandbag, the rifle stock firm and steady on the other.

"Here they come," Sam said. "Four hundred meters for the limousine."

"Got it," Jamie Berenger said.

"Three hundred meters now," Sam said.

"Got it," Jamie Berenger said.

"Closing on the point of aim," Sam said.

Two seconds later, the sound of the big rifle boomed throughout the valley. The muzzle lifted off the fore-end sandbag a good six inches and fire shot out the slits in the muzzle brake. Before Sam could recover from the blast, Jamie Berenger had cycled the bolt, extracted the spent round, put it in a pocket, and, with his cheek glued to the stock of the rifle, waited to be fed the second round. Sam put it in his hand like a nurse handing a scalpel to a surgeon. Jamie Berenger chambered the round and rammed the big bolt home.

When the bullet hit the limousine, a huge cloud of smoke, debris, and fire exploded into view and then disappeared behind another dense cloud of smoke and destruction. When the smoke cleared, the limousine was turned sideways. What remained of the front pointed directly at the concrete barrier on the right hand side of the road. The big bullet had hit the engine block at the midpoint. A half-pound of solid brass traveling at 2800 feet per second penetrated the 700-pound engine block through and through and shattered it on impact. The engine, reacting to the pressures of the huge bullet ripping through its middle, instantly became a 700-pound bomb containing a million shards of cast iron, steel and aluminum exploding through the firewall, the fenders and the hood at supersonic speeds. This explosion obliterated the entire front section of the car and the two people sitting there.

After the smoke cleared, one could see that the limousine no longer had a front seat, although two lengths of twisted steel, which were the remains of the frame, stuck out the front and were jammed into the concrete barrier. Smoke rolled from underneath the chassis of the ruined car and what remained of the rear portion of the car. The windows appeared to have been blown out the smoldering passenger compartment and there was no sign of movement.

The rifle boomed again after the chase car pulled up to the wreckage and men jumped out with submachine guns at the ready, running toward the limousine, presumably to rescue the director. As the men approached the car, the second round, which was aimed at the trunk area of the limousine, ruptured the fuel tank. What was left of the Lincoln erupted in a fiery explosion engulfing the three agents in flames. The driver of the chase car spun his wheels backing away from his flaming comrades. The chase car was still spinning its tires in reverse gear when it crashed into one of the police motorcycles, knocking the policeman one way and the cycle another. The runaway Suburban bumped over the downed motorcycle and then smashed into a car that had stopped on the parkway, ending the Suburban's flight to safety.

The three agents, covered in fire, ran around like figures in a cartoon flapping their arms and falling over each other. Two of them fired all the rounds in their submachine guns as if that would help extinguish the fire that was burning them alive. Bullets spattered and pinged off the wreckage, the road, the concrete barriers and even the Suburban they had just been riding in. Agents from the lead car, who were now running back to the wreckage, dived to the ground for cover. By the time they got to their burning comrades, the burned men were dead, as were all the passengers of the limousine, including the Director of the BATF.

Meanwhile, drivers traveling in the opposite direction on the Parkway, although separated by concrete Jersey barriers, could see clearly the fiery conflagration on the other side of the road, and as cars stopped to rubberneck at the unbelievable spectacle, other cars rammed into them, and then still other cars rammed into those cars, until multiple vehicle fires were in full blaze, and cars skidded at every angle trying to avoid the cars stopped in front of them. Within minutes, traffic was stopped for miles on both sides of the parkway.

"Feed me," Jamie Berenger said. He had carefully ejected the second round and put it in his velcroed cargo pants pocket along with the first. Sam gave him a third round.

This time, the bullet hit the lead escort car. When the limousine crashed into the concrete barrier, the lead car had screeched to a stop and done a Y turn in the middle of the parkway, speeding back to the stricken limousine. It was now facing away from Jamie Berenger and pointing toward the limousine it was supposed to be protecting. Three of its occupants stood helpless near the burned out wreckage and the driver remained in the Suburban. Jamie Berenger fired the third round into the roof of the remaining Suburban about a foot back from the windscreen. The bullet penetrated the roof, ripping through the front passenger compartment, exploding the windscreen, and again hitting the engine block. This time, the impact was to the rear of the block, and the ensuing explosion of the engine sent shrapnel through the firewall of the car and everywhere else on a 360 degree axis, killing the driver instantly. Within seconds, fuel dripping from the open fuel line caught fire and the wreckage of the lead car was also engulfed in flames.

Jamie Berenger carefully ejected the third round and put the empty casing in his side pocket.

"I think we're done," he said.

Plainly wearied by the exertion, he got up slowly and surveyed the destruction below.

"Take the mat," Sam said. "I got everything else."

Jamie Berenger rolled up the mat and hobbled off the railroad trestle more slowly than he had come on.

19

Following the death of the director of BATF, the government mounted a massive campaign of mourning, outrage, appeal to morality, and a call for swift justice. For the most part, editorial writers across the country agreed. One could not mask murder by assuming the cloak of the patriot. In fact, a patriot was a person who loved the land he lived in and was a partner with the government in making a better life for everyone. The insistence of the government on its moral superiority seemed infectious and began to be regurgitated by newscasters, talk show hosts, and documentaries on the good work done by BATF.

The first sign of trouble came on the internet when some brave sole created a blog suggesting that the glut of media coverage of the BATF shootings was disinformation. Others picked up on the idea, and then a newspaper in Burlington, Vermont suggested that the government case may have been overblown. Small papers in Florida, Montana, and Washington then echoed that thought. Things really got rolling when two women who had resigned from BATF put forward the claim that the former director of BATF was an alcoholic, womanizing, small-minded, and, in fact, stupid political appointee. One of the women was a victim of the director's amorous affections, and was suing him, and the other was a high-ranking officer who had defended the other woman's protests and was herself fired. Both women appeared on national television and a sea swell of anger developed about the whole process of political appointees becoming the heads of agencies and having no qualifications for the jobs.

Following this were web sites and blogs questioning the portrayal of the BATF as heroes who protected the homeland. Ruby Ridge and Wako were resurrected and seemed to generate the inquiry: why did the BATF have to attack citizens with a military force rather than just ask them if they could come in and examine their guns. And how did it make sense to amass a military force anyway when the target was an individual?

Editorial writers began to pick up some of these questions and the whole question of civil disobedience was raised. Dr. Martin Luther King had counseled the breaking of laws to achieve a greater good, and had also advised that if one is going to do that, one has to be willing to go to jail. But was killing the BATF agents civil disobedience, or just murder? Nationally syndicated columns appeared on the subject and polls were conducted which tended to show that people were evenly divided on the question of whether Aaron 's actions, as reported in the press, were justifiable protest or murder. The government was alarmed.

At this point, pockets of anger seemed to appear all over the country. People of all types began to come out and suggest that maybe Aaron was a patriot. The country was formed, after all, when a king became an oppressor and citizens armed with rifles resisted. Isn't that what the BATF had become, and wasn't the BATF just the cat's paw for the government?

Hoping the quell this tide of anger, the U.S. Attorney for the WHoping the quell this tide of anger, the U.S. Attorney for the Western District of Pennsylvania was directed by the White House to prosecute Aaron immediately. The U.S. Attorney was called directly by White House Counsel, on the phone jointly with the Chief of Staff. "The President wants this done. Now. No delays." Aaron's case was set down for a preliminary hearing, and he was represented by Bradford Hayes.

At the preliminary hearing, Aaron was charged with murder, treason, violating the civil rights of federal law enforcement officers, conspiracy, and committing a crime with a ethnic motivation (Corky James was Irish).

A stern veteran agent, Myron Blount, who had been in charge of Aaron 's interrogation following his arrest, testified for the government. The entirety of the government's case was that Aaron confessed that he had killed both ATF agents. Attorney Hayes conducted the cross-examination.

"Agent Blount," he began, "I was surprised that you did not include in your case against Aaron that he killed the Director of BATF."

"Aaron was in custody when the Director was killed."

"So someone else killed him?"

"Obviously."

"Could that person have killed these other agents as well?"

"No. Aaron , as I said, confessed to those killings."

"Was he seen at either crime scene?"

"No."

"Did you lift his fingerprints from the weapons used?"

"We never found the weapons."

"Did you lift his fingerprints from anything at the crime scene?"

"No."

"Did you find items belonging to the victim in his possession?"

"No."

"Did you find materials, tools, books, papers, guns, or anything at his house that would suggest he was involved in these killings?"

"No."

"Did you interview Aaron's neighbors and others who knew him?"

"Yes."

"Did any of those persons express a concern about things Aaron had told them suggesting that he would, indeed, have committed these killings?"

"No."

"You say that you found no guns?"

"Correct."

"How did Aaron kill these men without guns?"

"He may have worked with confederates. They may have the guns."

"Did he tell you that?"

"No."

"Do you have evidence of that beyond a surmise?"

"No."

"Isn't it unbelievable that an eighty-one year old man could commit these crimes?"

"It is unusual."

"Does it raise any questions in your mind?'

"No."

"If it is so unusual, why does it not raise questions?"

"Because he said he did it."

"When you arrested Aaron , did he resist?"

"No."

"Why was he in the hospital for three weeks after the arrest, then?"

"He's an old man."

"Wasn't it because ATF agents dressed in full battle gear knocked him down and beat him intro unconsciousness?"

"I wasn't at the arrest."

"But you know about the arrest?"

"Yes."

"Isn't it true that over two hundred agents were used to arrest this man?"

"No."

"No?"

"No. There were two men."

"Oh, so two hundred agents were used to arrest two men."

"Yes."

"Isn't this precisely what the ATF killer is protesting?"

"Well, Aaron is the ATF killer, and I have no idea what he's protesting."

"Really? You were in charge of the interrogation of Aaron, were you not?"

"Yes."

"Then how could you not know what his alleged purpose was?"

"I didn't care what his purpose was. I just cared whether he did it."

"And what was your conclusion?"

"He did it."

"Based on. . . ."

"Based on his confession."

"Agent Blount, have you ever heard of corpus delicti?"

"Yeah, it means something like the body of the crime."

"What is that?"

"Objection. Calls for expertise outside of the agent's competence."

"Sustained."

"When you investigate crimes, you usually look for evidence of criminal activity, don't you?"

"Yes."

"Did you look for evidence of criminal activity in this case?"

"Yes."

"What did you do?"

"We searched Aaron 's house, we talked to his neighbors and people who said they knew him, we searched his employment records, we went to his synagogue, we dug up his back yard, and we talked to him."

"And after that massive effort, you ended up with what?"

"A confession," Blount said, smugly.

"Would it be correct to say that in most cases you have been involved in that there is evidence of criminal activity in addition to a confession, or even evidence without a confession?"

Blount thought for a time and then said, "Yes."

"There is usually evidence beyond the confession?"

"Yes."

"Why is that?"

"Objection. Beyond his competence."

"Overruled."

"Why is that?"

"Because it's there, so it's part of the case."

"But in this case there is no evidence beyond the confession?"

"Correct."

"Just so we're clear, I'll repeat. There is no evidence beyond the confession?"

"Correct."

"No further questions, Your Honor."

"Any redirect, Ms. Adams?"

"No, Your Honor."

"Your Honor," Hayes said, "at this point I move for a dismissal. There is no corpus delicti. The Supreme Court has written. . . give me just a moment. . ." Hayes leafed through his notes and finally came up with the right paper. "The Supreme Court has written:

To avoid the injustice of a conviction where no crime exists, the law has adopted a rule of caution which holds that the corpus delicti must be proven before a conviction can stand. This is emphasized where the state's case depends on a confession by defendant.

"Your Honor, this rule requires that before there can be a criminal conviction, the government must have something more than a confession.

"In other words, to successfully prosecute a criminal case, the government must have evidence independent of any confession that a crime has been committed. If, for example, Jane Doe confesses that she murdered John Doe, the state must have something beyond the confession in order to prevail. There must, for example, be evidence that John Doe died in such a way that a criminal act caused his death.

"Here, nothing beyond the confession was presented, and the case, must, therefore, be dismissed.

"Ms. Adams?"

"Your Honor, I'm surprised by this argument. I would request a continuance in order to do some research on the point. Perhaps both sides could present Your Honor with a memorandum of law on the subject."

"It's pretty straightforward isn't it?" the judge said.

"Ahhhhh"

"Your Honor, there is no need for research on this point. The law is clear. In fact, it's hornbook law, as Ms. Smith well knows. The truth is that the government just doesn't have a case, and I renew my motion."

"Ms. Adams?"

"Your Honor, if Mr. Hayes' argument is that we should have put on evidence that the two deaths were not the result of natural causes, but that they resulted from a crime, we can easily put that on."

"Now?" the court said.

"No, Your Honor. I don't have this material with me, but I can easily get it if you will allow me a continuance to go back to my office."

"Your Honor," Hayes said. "The witness testified, without objection, that there is no evidence in the case except for the confession. For that reason alone, my motion should be granted."

"Ms. Adams. You have wasted everyone's time with your slipshod presentation of this case. If the government decides that it wants to bring the prosecution again, next time with the proper evidence, it may do so. In the meantime, he case is dismissed. Mr. Silverman, you are free to go."

Outside, on the street, cheers began to go up. The case was being broadcast live on public radio. Aaron shook Bradford Hayes' hand. The prosecution looked distressed. BATF agents in the courtroom were barely able to contain their rage. Leaving his papers behind, Bradford Hayes whisked Aaron out of the courtroom as best he could, pushing through the crowds of well-wishers.

20

When Aaron and Hayes came out of the federal courthouse onto Grant Street, a huge crowd had gathered. Police later estimated that at least five thousand people had gathered on Grant Street, spilling over onto Liberty Avenue and stretching into downtown. Traffic was at a standstill. The streets were wall-to-wall people with no cars in sight. Police efforts to move people off the streets and onto the sidewalk were futile.

A loud roar went up when Hayes and Aaron stepped out the door. Someone had brought a six-foot stepladder, and people helped the old man climb it so that the crowd could see him better. As he reached the top of the ladder and waved, the entire crowd threw caps and confetti and newspapers into the air. Some people released balloons and the cheers were deafening.

At length, Aaron was helped down from the ladder and Hayes managed to move him through the crowd toward the strip district. As he passed through the people, hands reached out to touch him. The voices were everywhere: "We love you." "Give 'em hell." "A true patriot," "We're with you, Aaron."

The old man was virtually exhausted by the time Hayes got him to a pre-arranged spot near the strip where Sam and Hayes were able to get him into the Landcruiser. He closed his eyes and dozed off on the way home.

"Good Job, Bradford," Sam said.

"It's just a stop-gap. As soon as the U.S. Attorney gets back to her office, she'll draw up new criminal charges and they'll arrest him all over again. Next time, she'll put in the forensic evidence that the deaths were caused by criminal activity, and he'll be held over for trial. I'm really concerned about how much of this he can take," Hayes said.

"I know," Sam said. "Is there any way you can prevent her from filing again?"

"No. The judge dismissed because their case was deficient, but they can always file again and fix the deficiency since the dismissal came at the preliminary hearing stage. There is no double jeopardy because a jury was not sworn in."

"Why didn't he just let her walk back to her office and get the coroners' reports or whatever it was she needed to establish that the deaths were from criminal acts?" Sam said.

"He could have," Hayes said. "I think he was just pissed off that she didn't do it right the first time. Actually, I think what happened is that whoever is pushing this case pushed her too fast to get into court, and she just got caught up in the fact that she had a confession. She forgot what she needed. Also she probably didn't expect me to put up such a fight at the preliminary hearing since he's so obviously guilty. She probably thought that the whole defense would be that he's an old man fighting oppression."

Sam's cell phone rang. It was Nick.

"Sam, I'm over at Aaron 's house. There are people everywhere. I don't think you could even drive in here. I saw the crowd downtown on T.V., and it's just like that here. There have to be several thousand people."

"O.K. Nick. Does anyone seem to be in charge?"

"I don't really know. There are some guys with megaphones that seem to be organizing things."

"I'll take Aaron to my house. He's passed out in the back seat right now. We'll get him rested up and fed. Why don't you see if you can locate some leaders in the crowd and tell them we'll take Aaron someplace big, probably outside, about 5:00 this afternoon. That will give him a chance to rest."

"You want me to work out where we can go?"

"Yeah. And get the leaders to publicize it somehow," Sam said.

Sam and Hayes led the sleepy old man into Sam's den, took his shoes off, and put him on the couch with a thick comforter. He was asleep as soon as the comforter covered him up.

Nick called back within an hour. "We've got a committee of people who are coordinating things," he said. "And we've chosen that big hill behind the skating rink at Schenley Park. Somebody said it will hold ten thousand people."

"Sounds good, Nick. But how will anyone know about this?"

"I don't think there will be any problems. One of the coordinators just put it on the internet and word is spreading by cell phone. I think the place is going to be mobbed. How's our boy?"

"He's asleep right now. He'll be o.k. by this afternoon."

"O.K. I'm going to stay around here and work with these people so we know what they're doing."

"We'll see you this afternoon."

Sam and Hayes got some rest themselves and then got Aaron up around three for a shower and a hot meal.

"I really appreciate all you both have done for us," Aaron said, beginning his second grilled cheese sandwich."

"You know you're quite a celebrity," Hayes said. "There's going to be a huge gathering of people at five this afternoon, and they'll be waiting to see you."

"I don't have anything to say," the old man said

"You don't have to talk," Sam said. "You're a symbol of resistance to government oppression, and they love you for that. They just want to see you and be reassured that you actually exist."

"You know, I'm just an old man. I feel bad about killing those agents."

"No sane man likes killing," Sam said. "It's a burden you will have to bear. Sometimes it has to be done."

"I know that. But I didn't expect it t be so hard to do this."

"It will get harder," Hayes said. "They will arrest you again and re-charge you. When they do that, I don't know whether I can keep you out of jail or not."

"I expected that," the old man said. "It's all right. I'll be all right. It was something we had to do." He finished his sandwich and then a bowl of chili and a glass of milk.

At four-thirty, Sam pulled the Landcruiser into Shenley Park. Aaron was in the back and Bradford Hayes was in front. As he approached the park, traffic was snarled, and hordes of people appeared everywhere. Nick had arranged with the organizers to have people meet Sam's truck and escort it through the crowds. Otherwise, he'd never make it to the top of the hill.

The distance from the Boulevard of the Allies to the top of the hill in Schenley Park was about a mile, but halfway up the hill, the crowds on the road were simply too dense to move aside, and so Sam drove on the grass, slowly progressing through crowds of well-wishers who touched the old man's hands as he leaned out the window and they slowly climbed the hill.

At the top of the hill a makeshift stage-heavy planks on tall stepladders-had been erected. If Aaron were able to climb up there, he would be about seven feet above the ground and thousands of people could see him. A makeshift loudspeaker system had also been set up. Sam and Hayes met with the extemporaneous leaders while Aaron sat in the back of the Landcruiser handing out autographs.

Somewhere out in the crowd of ten to fifteen thousand Jesse and Jamie Berenger mingled with the young people. There was a lot of talk about who this old man was and how he could have pulled this off. Everyone admired his courage. Jesse and Jamie Berenger said nothing.

Once Aaron had been arrested, Sam instructed Jesse and Jamie Berenger to stay away from Aaron. It seemed likely that if the BATF found out they were friends, they would arrest them also, or at the very least, secure search warrants for their houses.

"This is hard to believe," Jamie Berenger said.

"You got that right. I never seen so many people," Jesse said, munching on a sandwich. People handed the old men sandwiches and cold drinks as they walked around, and everyone seemed friendly.

21

Back at the federal building, the U.S. Attorney was barking orders. The new criminal information was finished and a trio of Assistant U.S. Attorneys were taking an arrest warrant for Aaron Silverman to a judge for approval. Sixteen cars of BATF, FBI and Internal Revenue agents sat in the federal building parking garage waiting for the arrest warrant.

Meanwhile, two cars of BATF agents sat several blocks from Aaron 's house, watching the crowd. Earlier in the day, Nick had opened the house for the organizers and invited them to use the facilities as needed. The crime scene tape had been torn down and people filed in and out of the house for water and the bathrooms. Although it had been announced throughout the day that Aaron would appear at Schenley Park in the late afternoon, many people elected to stay at Aaron 's house, some because they had no transportation to the park, others because they expected the old man to return home after the park. They could see him then.

The assault team leader in the sixteen-car convoy radioed the agents sitting near Aaron 's house.

"Have you seen the target yet?"

"Negative. There are several thousand people mingling around the house and the neighborhood, but no sign of the old man."

"Could he be in the house?"

"He could be. We couldn't get here right away because of the crowd."

"I'd like you to go up to the house and see if he's there. It will probably take all of us to arrest him, but you should be able at least to find out if he is there."

"I'll get back to you."

The agent, who had been talking on the radio got out of his unmarked black Mercury and, joined by his partner, began walking toward the house.

Two other agents stayed in their separate car. As the agents began walking the two blocks down a hill to the house, the crowds got thicker. People were seated on the streets, some playing guitars, some just lying in the sun, others talking in small groups. Some neighbors invited the crowd to use their yards, and had set up card tables containing large water jugs and paper cups. One woman was sitting at a card table making peanut butter sandwiches.

The agents stuck out in the crowd not only because of their dark suits, but also because of the way they carried themselves, like bulldogs in a poodle show, with a thinly disguised aggressiveness. They seemed to have contempt for the crowd. The crowd got dense as they neared the house, and it took them nearly half an hour to push through the crowd and get to the house. By then, it was apparent that everyone who saw them knew who they were.

At the back door of the house, the lead agent encountered one of the extempore organizers and said, "Is Aaron Silverman in there?"

"Who wants to know?" the man said.

"BATF," the agent said, showing his identification.

"Nooooooooooo. You don't say," the man said.

"Is he?"

"Why don't you just get the hell out of here?" the man said.

"Get out of the way," the agent said.

"You guys are pretty good at beatin up old men. Why don't you try some of us?"

"You are under arrest. Tom, put the cuffs on him," the agent said.

The agents were standing on the lawn below the kitchen door two steps below the man who was talking to them. When the agent with the cuffs approached the man at the door, the man simply threw out his right leg and kicked the agent in the face. The kicker was well over two hundred pounds, and the agent fell backwards on the grass stunned, with a bloody nose.

The first agent stepped back in a crouch and drew his gun, but before he could say anything, he was mobbed from behind by five large men and went down beneath their collective weight. As soon as he hit the ground, there was the sound of a muffled gunshot.

Slowly, the men piled off the agent, and when the last man was off, the agent remained still on the ground. Someone rolled him over and there was a large contact bullet wound in his upper chest. He had fallen on his gun and discharged it into his chest.

The other agent was just now regaining his feet and looked at the fallen agent in horror and fear. When he got to his feet, he began running, pushing his way through the crowd, heading back to his car. Suddenly, he was in a bad dream. His partner was dead. They were going to kill him. His life was over. How could it happen so fast? What had happened, anyway? He pushed and shoved and scrambled through the dense crowd, but he never seemed to get anywhere. "They're gonna kill me," he hallucinated," then scrambled even faster, falling, crawling, running, sure that the murderers were on his trail.

Because he was crashing into people and stepping on legs and arms of those seated on the ground, people began shoving him back, and finally, he stumbled and sprawled on the street. People began to move back from him, and then a circle formed around him. The agent jumped up in a panic. He dove headlong into the crowd and ran in the direction of the car.

The crowd gradually thinned out and the agent, who was by now completely disheveled, was able to see behind him, looking as he stumbled and ran. No one seemed to be following. Then he saw the other car, and as he approached, the other two agents got out.

"What the hell happened? Where's John?" one said.

Breathless and hyperventilating, Tom said, "They killed him. I barely got away."

"Who killed him?"

"Those people. The mob. The ones at the house. They just jumped on him and I heard a shot and when they got off him, he was dead."

"Where were you?"

"I was on the ground. Some guy kicked me and knocked me down."

"Why didn't they kill you?"

"I don't know. I guess John must have drawn his gun when they kicked me and then they jumped him. There were five or six men on him."

"We gotta call this in," one of the agents said, turning back and getting in the car.

At the federal building, the agent with the arrest warrant was just getting in the lead car when the call came in from the agents at Aaron's house.

"John's dead?" the assault team leader said. "Can you get to him? What the hell? Can you retrieve the body?"

"I don't think so," the agent in the car said. "The crowd seems to be getting riled up. They seem to be moving toward us, and we're about two blocks from the house."

"Can you maintain your position until we get there?" the assault team leader said.

Because of the approaching wall of people, the other two agents got in the car. One agent started it up.

"I don't think so," the agent said. "A whole army of people is approaching us. We gotta get out of here."

The driver threw the car in reverse and backed up the street away from the crowd. Two blocks away, he reached a cross street, and quickly turned into it and sped away from the crowd.

The agent in the passenger seat called the team leader at the federal building. "We just narrowly escaped the crowd. You're gonna need several hundred riot equipped agents to get John's body out of there."

"Report back here. We'll get an assault force together."

Meanwhile, several members of the crowd had tried to give the fallen agent emergency first aid. Finally, a doctor was located in the crowd, and after repeated efforts to revive the agent, he gave up and pronounced the agent dead.

As he did, a fire truck pulled up in front of the house. It could barely be seen over the crowd that had pressed against the house. When they saw the fire truck, the first aid givers lifted the agent's body onto a blanket and four men carried him through the crowd to the waiting fire truck.

The crowd parted to allow the blanket bearers through, and when they reached the fire truck, they gently lowered the body to the ground. The doctor spoke to the fire captain. "I'm a doctor. We tried to give first aid and revive him, but he didn't respond. He died of a gunshot wound."

The fire captain got out of the truck and said, "o.k., doc. An Ambulance is right behind us. Are these people going to cause trouble when we take this guy out of here?"

"I don't think so. As far as I can tell, this shooting was an accident. I don't think anyone here wanted to kill this man."

The ambulance slowly wound through the crowd and stopped behind the fire truck. The firemen stayed in the truck and the fire captain went back to talk to the ambulance driver. Several men in the crowd picked up the body of the agent and carried him back to the ambulance. The paramedics lifted the body onto a stretcher, closed the doors, and followed the fire truck slowly through the crowd. The crowd parted to allow the vehicles through and there was a hushed quiet as they passed.

At the federal building, the assault team leader was waiting for SWAT personnel from various federal agencies to respond to his call for help in retrieving the body of a fallen federal agent. He tapped his fingers impatiently waiting for the FBI to notify him that their people were in place. As he was impatiently waiting, a radio call came in for him.

"We have just received notice from the city that they have picked up the body of agent Sullivan. He is being taken to Presbyterian Hospital. He was pronounced dead at the scene by a doctor who was there."

"How in the hell did the city get in there?"

"A fire truck and an ambulance just drove in," the dispatcher said. "They said the people helped them put the body of agent Sullivan in the ambulance."

"Anything else?"

"Yes. The city tells us that there is a huge gathering at Schenley Park. They believe it is Aaron. They say that various roads in the area may have to be closed and that there are in excess of ten thousand people gathered on the grounds of the park. They are monitoring the situation from the air."

Within twenty minutes, a convoy of twenty-seven federal vehicles, including an armored truck, five SWAT trucks, and an armored personnel carrier, headed toward Schenley Park. The park was only eight miles from the federal building.

When the first federal cars in the convoy got to the bridge over Panther Hollow on Boulevard of the Allies they were stopped both by city police and by the density of the crowd.

"We are going through there," the assault leader said to the policeman. "Move your barricades."

"My orders are that no one goes through," the policeman said.

"This is a federal matter. I'm in control here and I'm telling you to move your barrier."

"I'm sorry, sir, but you'll have to talk with my commander."

The federal assault leader got on the radio to the armored personnel carrier. "Go through the barriers," he said. "Run them down. We'll be right behind you. If they don't get out of the way, run over them."

The two armored vehicles steered out of their places in line and approached the police barriers. Two policemen stood in their path.

"What do we do, sir?" the armored truck radioed.

"Run them over," the assault leader fumed.

The armored truck started slowly in creeper gear, and with the armored personnel carrier on its tail, crushed the barriers and forced the policemen aside. The policemen jumped out of the way and shouted frantically into their radios as the long procession of federal cars continued on through the crowd, which parted slowly as the menacing trucks approached.

About halfway up the hill, the crowd began banging on the sides of the cars and trucks in the federal convoy. The park was so dense with people that they were pressed against the cars and it seemed impossible to even open the doors of the cars. When the lead truck got three quarters way up the hill and the driver could see the scaffolding on which Aaron now stood waving at the crowd, it stopped and the men in the federal convoy pushed their way out of the cars and trucks.

There were a hundred seventy-five uniformed, helmeted, vested, rifle-toting officers. They pushed their way into the crowd and were ordered to form a skirmish line facing the scaffolding. The crowd was pressed against them so densely that it took half an hour to spread out in a line facing the top of the hill. Once the men finally got into position, it seemed to them that this was a tactical disaster waiting to happen. If things went bad, they would be mobbed from all directions. But BATF was adamant. This is how it would be done. There would be a skirmish line and it would push its way up to the scaffold, arrest Aaron, and bring him back to the convoy.

By the time a hundred seventy-five armed, battle dressed, helmeted agents got spread out across the field leading to the scaffold, it was apparent to everyone in the crowd that the line of agents was going to push through to the scaffold-stage and do something to Aaron. It seemed most likely that they would either shut him down or arrest him. The lead assault agent for BATF was shouting something in a megaphone about "federal officers" and "arrest warrant." After that, the crowd didn't push as easily and stood nose to nose with the advancing line of officers. The skirmish line slowed as the resistance increased. Also, the crowd behind the officers pushed them from behind. They were sandwiched front and back.

Then the inevitable happened. One of the agents panicked from the tension and the claustrophobia and fired his carbine in the air. It was a three shot burst. Five hundred people in the immediate area fell to the ground, believing that the shooting had begun and the agents intended to kill them all.

Within seconds, the mood of the crowd turned angry. "So you want to kill us, you fuckers," came a cry, and a twenty-five foot length of the crowd surged into the officers at the mid-point of the skirmish line, and forced them back into the crowd behind them. There were struggles for weapons, and a whole segment of the police line disappeared, swarmed by the overwhelming numbers of the crowd. Now and then a man emerged holding an assault rifle or a submachine gun above his head in victory, and then disappeared into the masses.

On the ground, the agents were kicked unmercifully. Some of them were suffocating under three or four bodies. In an effort to help their fallen comrades, both ends of the police line turned inwards toward the breach, and began butt stroking and clubbing anyone who was close enough to be hit. The skirmish line no longer existed. Instead, it had become two lines of police turning inward toward the middle of the line, which had been overrun.

Then on the left, there were shots. It was a burst of machine gun fire followed immediately by screams and a roar of outrage and by people running for safety away from the point of conflict.

As the crowd ran to either end of the advancing police lines in fear for their lives, the officers continued their pincer movement toward their fallen comrades. The crowd was being squeezed between the two advancing lines of police, and when it began to thin, there was room to see. . . . .and to shoot.

Twelve rifles and submachine guns had been ripped from the hands of fallen officers and the men who held these weapons were trapped between the advancing lines of the pincer movement. The two advancing lines moved toward each other and toward those unfortunates who remained between them. Suddenly, gunfire erupted from the people trapped between the advancing police lines. Those holding the assault rifles and submachine guns torn from the downed officers had opened fire on the police.

This was a total surprise to the officers who still had their weapons, for they knew that their comrades were down, but not that some of them had been disarmed. Nonetheless, return fire was almost immediate. It was also undisciplined. Instead of firing at those who were assaulting them, the police fired their weapons on full auto at the crowd at large, apparently forgetting that their own comrades were facing them in the line of fire.

Waves of people trapped between the two lines of police began to fall, and others kept running toward the ends of the advancing police lines and were able to escape only because the police shot their magazines dry. The police fell too, sometimes from adversarial fire, sometimes from the friendly fire of their comrades who were facing them. Forty-two officers and all twelve civilians armed with police rifles lay dead after shooting ended.

As the crowd ran both in front of them and behind them, the police looked for direction and responded to orders to close ranks, leaving their stricken comrades on the ground unattended. They reformed the skirmish line, not in the pincer movement facing each other, but again facing the scaffold on which Aaron stood, and they advanced up the hill.

When the lead BATF agent saw that the way to the scaffold had cleared, he rallied what was left of his team, and they ran toward the scaffold ahead of the skirmish line. But around the scaffold a circle of men four rows deep had formed shoulder to shoulder. Aaron stood high up on the plank of the scaffolding. As the sixteen ATF agents approached the scaffolding at a run, the reformed police line of approximately a hundred remaining officers from various agencies advanced at a walk, the bodies of their fallen comrades and of members of the crowd lay behind them. Now they were unopposed.

When the lead ATF agent approached the men circling the scaffolding, he held up his arrest warrant and yelled, "You men. Disburse. I have an arrest warrant for Aaron Silverman. If you resist, I will shoot." The head agent's face was red and spittle was spraying from his mouth as he yelled at the protective circle. "Move you bastards," he screamed.

The men did not move, but Aaron turned his back on the agent and began slowly to move toward the ladder end of the scaffolding to descend. He knew that he needed to give up, to present himself for arrest, to save his supporters from more violence. Apparently incensed that the protective circle would not move, the lead agent began to fire his handgun in the air. Then he caught Aaron 's movement in his peripheral vision, spun on his heel, and fired at the retreating figure nine times. He hit Aaron in the side and the back five times. The men in the protective circle stared in disbelief, and then an angry roar went up and the protective circle surged as if it were a single organism.

Instantly, the sixteen BATF agents were overwhelmed. The agents fired into the surging crowd and a dozen attackers dropped, mortally wounded, but the ATF agents were overrun and buried under several layers of angry attackers by the time the advancing police line got to them and started clubbing members of the protective circle and dragging them off their comrades. When the attackers were pulled off the BATF agents, all sixteen agents were dead of suffocation, stab wounds, and blows to the head or gunshots.

A hundred twelve members of the protective circle were subdued and arrested, including Sam and Nick, who were standing under the scaffolding. Nick caught the body of Aaron as he tumbled from the plank on which he had been standing. Nick sat on the grass holding Aaron's head in his lap. Aaron's shirt was stained red front and back from the bullets that had ended his life. Thirty-seven of the protectors lay dead. Scattered over the hill leading up to the scaffold, another 195 civilians lay dead.

22

This time BATF was not receptive to Naratova's phone call, and he had to appear in person to spring Sam and Nick from the federal lockup. Naratova waited until they got to the exit door of the federal building before he donned his signature baseball cap. Sam and Nick followed him out the side door onto Grant Street, somewhat tense from having been hassled by the BATF for the last six hours.

"Is there a place around here we could have something to eat," Naratova said.

"Yeah," Sam said, "Walk up a block on Grant and then turn right a block. There's a bagel place there on the corner."

The three men started walking. "What the fuck do you guys think you're doing, anyway?" Naratova said. "I tell you to make sure we don't have any citizen revolts and the next thing I know you guys are in the middle of the biggest goddam citizen revolt since 1776."

Sam led the way into the restaurant and got a booth for three. They ordered coffee and eggs.

"Look Gregory," Sam said. "We didn't have any way to know this was going to happen. We took Aaron out to that field to solidify his identity as a folk hero."

"Why in the hell did you want to do that?"

"Because that is how we planned to control this thing. The plan was that Aaron would become the figurehead for the anti-BATF movement and then when he would tell people to cool it, they would recognize him as the leader and do what he said."

"Well, now they've killed him," Naratova said. "So where does that leave you. How are you going to control things now?"

"Aaron wasn't in this alone," Sam said.

"He wasn't?"

"No, there are two other old men who worked with him. His buddies."

"Jesus. What are these guys trying to do?"

"Oddly, the same thing you are trying to do. Get rid of the BATF."

"No doubt because they believe in freedom and justice for all."

"You got it, Naratova. That's what they believe in. They don't know about multi-national corporations and unmarked bags of money. They stick with the old timey stuff. Not your cup of tea, I know, but that's what they think."

"World War II veterans?"

"Yeah."

"Old guys?"

"Yeah."

"How are you gonna use them?"

"We're gonna put them in the place of Aaron . They'll be the new folk heroes."

"How are you gonna do that?"

"Not sure yet."

"Why will anybody listen to them?"

"Because they're old guys just like Aaron who stand for the same things he stood for."

"And if they're accepted as the new heroes?"

"Then I think all we have to do is point out that the BATF kills people like Aaron and his buddies. That should make the BATF unpopular."

"The BATF is already unpopular."

"Yes, they are unpopular, but that unpopularity has never before been channeled into political action."

"Why would it manifest itself in political action now?"

"Because for the first time there is a unifying figure—a reason to act. They killed Aaron and now they need to be dealt with."

"It seems to me that you're flirting with civil war," Naratova said.

"You said it yourself, Gregory. The reason you're upset with the BATF is that they are flirting with civil war. The people just want to be left alone."

"You just make sure that it works out that way. We do not want these guys in the streets with their hunting rifles. We do not, I repeat Sam, want that."

"There's a wild card," Sam said "The bozos who run ATF and the bigger bozos they report to are capable of almost anything. Look at what they just did. I'll keep this under control unless they spiral it out of control. They can do that, Gregory, and I can't prevent them from doing it."

"I don't care what they do Sam. I only care what you do. Now, please, don't make me fly out here again to spring you out of jail."

* * *

Headlines in the Post Gazette were: *"Thousands Gather to Attend Aaron Silverman's Funeral."* The story continued:

> *Aaron Silverman, an eighty-one year old veteran of World War II, was killed yesterday by police gunfire as he stood on a makeshift stage in Schenley Park, where more than ten thousand people had gathered to hear him speak. Earlier in the day federal murder charges against him had been dismissed. Trouble erupted when approximately two hundred federal police officers charged into the crowd in an effort to re-arrest Silverman on new charges after he had been released.*
>
> *Today, the Pittsburgh International Airport confirms that record numbers of passengers have arrived from all over the country, apparently to attend Silverman's funeral. Local hotels report that they are full, as do motels in a fifty-mile radius, and grassroots organizations offering free rooms in private homes have sprung up across the city. Numerous churches have opened their doors and church congregations have also organized free rooms for those who need them.*

Because of the unprecedented numbers of people who arrived in Pittsburgh to attend Aaron 's memorial service, Sam enlisted Naratova's aid in securing Heinz field for the service. Aaron 's body remained at the Schultz funeral home and would be buried later in the day.

By the time the memorial service started in the late morning, the 64,000 seats of Heinz Field were full and overflowing. People also stood on the sidewalks surrounding the stadium and watched the service on closed circuit television. Some of the major networks carried the memorial service live.

Opening the service was a rabbi, who said a prayer for the deceased. Following that was the playing of a recording of Samuel Barber's Adagio, Aaron 's favorite music. And following that, two old men took the podium, Jesse Washington and Jamie Berenger. They stood alone on the podium at the memorial service.

Jesse spoke first to the gathering of sixty-some thousand mourners. "Jamie Berenger and I are here because Aaron has been our friend for sixty years. We all served in the war together. And more recently, we served together in the protests we made to the Hitler-like tactics of the BATF. We asked the BATF the stop these tactics and to let some of their victims, particularly Clyde Mulhaney, go. They would not listen and we used the only weapon we had, we used our guns. Aaron surrendered to the BATF in an attempt to negotiate with them, but they arrested him instead. We did not surrender because we suspected they would do this and there had to be some of us left to keep this movement going."

There was a hushed murmur from the packed stadium. Jesse continued. "We are speaking now because we wish to honor our friend and because we want you to know that the movement that Aaron started has not ended with Aaron 's life."

Jamie Berenger then stood and addressed the crowd. "The things that we have been protesting and that all of you are protesting are getting worse. The BATF refuses to change its ways. Any student of history knows that the seizing of weapons is the first thing a dictatorial government does. That is now happening to us. Jesse and I are going to resist and we need your support. When we were young men, Aaron, Jesse and I saw what Hitler did in Europe. We saw what happened to people who could not defend themselves. We don't want that to happen here.

"We plan to once again ask the government to stop being a tyrant. Stop the seizing of guns. Stop invading people's houses with paramilitary police units. And if they will not, we then plan to publish the names and addresses of BATF agents in every office around the country. When that is done, we ask each of you who agrees with us to pick a name of an agent and start shooting. And you'll need to keep shooting until they give in.

"Of course, the newspapers will not publish our lists of names, but we will post them on the internet, and they will be easily accessible to all of you.

"Now that the BATF knows who we are and that we worked with Aaron, they will want to arrest us. We need to stay free at least long enough to get the government to stop being an oppressor. If we can get the government to stop collecting our weapons, and stop invading our homes with armies of thugs-oh, and to let Clyde Mulhaney go--we will surrender to the government and accept any punishment they choose to give us. But right now, we ask that you help us leave this place without being arrested. Goodbye and God bless you."

As Jesse Washington and Jamie Berenger left the podium, more than 64,000 people stood and cheered. The cheering went on for more than ten minutes after they had disappeared into an exit. Some of the same extemporaneous organizers who emerged the day before again took the podium and conducted prayers for Aaron and for everyone who would risk his life to oppose tyranny.

Following the service, for the next three hours, the crowd gradually left the stadium. Many people had picnics in the parking lot and along the river, which was near the stadium. Local restaurants on the north side and even in town were jammed. And among the crowd there was a friendliness, a sprit of camaraderie, and a joyousness of common purpose. A hope.

23

Following the massive memorial service for Aaron Silverman, the story of the Mulhaney case made national and international headlines. It was the constant subject of discussion on talk radio and in bars, restaurants and homes across the country. Not only that, but Congressional pressure was mounting for a presidential pardon. It was in this context that President Thurmond Fuller called a meeting of his cabinet. He had reluctantly agreed to make no comment on the public debate that had been raging, for his advisors convinced him that his anti-gun position would be likely to prevail if he remained silent and appeared to be neutral.

The President sat grim-faced at the head of a large conference table in the Roosevelt Room, the conference room across the hall from the Oval Office. In profile, the president looked somewhat like a television news anchor: carefully combed hair, aristocratic nose, face that was almost pretty. He impatiently tapped a pen on a yellow pad as the last of the cabinet members seated themselves at the table, their aides standing just behind them. In addition to members of the cabinet, the Chairman of the Joint Chiefs of Staff, the Director of the Bureau of Alcohol, Tobacco and Firearms, and the Director of the FBI were present. The mood was somber.

The Secretary of the Treasury, an old friend from the president's earlier career in Congress, sat next to the president on his right, and next to the Secretary, the new head of the BATF, who reported to the Treasury Secretary, looked somewhat out of place.

"Gentlemen," the president began, "I've limited this morning's agenda to the single issue of the recent murders of federal officers and the civil disobedience that has occurred in relation to those murders. I want this government to respond across the board and I want us all to be on the same page."

A murmur of assent rose from the Secretary of the Treasury and the head of the BATF.

The President continued, "An old man has conducted a killing spree against federal agents; more than a hundred federal agents are either dead or in the hospital on account of gun-related riots indirectly caused by that old man; two or three hundred civilians are dead or injured in the same riots; the old man is charged with crimes against federal officers and then is killed; tens of thousands of people attend the old man's funeral; and when more old men come forward and confess that they also had a part in killing federal agents, they are treated like heroes. This is insanity. How did events spiral into this carnage?"

The room was silent. Everyone in the room knew Thurmond Fuller was unfavorably disposed towards the private ownership of guns and also that he was unfavorably disposed towards those who opposed his view of private gun ownership.

Finally, the Attorney General said, "Mr. President, the old men you mentioned and the crowds that protested when one of the old men was shot by BATF agents saw themselves as defending liberty."

"That's nonsense," the president shot back, turning his whole body to toward the Attorney General. "How do you defend liberty by killing federal agents?"

"Sir," the Chairman of the Joint Chiefs said, "these people see themselves as defending the Constitution against events of the type that sparked all of this."

"What events are you talking about?" the president asked.

"The Mulhaney case."

"The Treasury Secretary and the director of the BATF briefed me on that some weeks ago." the president said.

"I wouldn't be too confident in the accuracy of that briefing," the Attorney General said.

"I resent that," Treasury Secretary O'Donnel said.

"He didn't have a machine gun," the general said. "He had a semi-auto rifle that malfunctioned."

"Now you wait a minute," the director of the BATF said. "It was a machine gun. You don't know the case. I do."

"I get intelligence reports," the general said. "And when you decided to invade this guy's house at four in the morning with a combat team, you made a big mistake. To the hundred-some-thousand people at that old man's funeral, you were behaving like jack-booted thugs."

"I resent that," the director of BATF said.

"You treated this case like the gun owner was getting ready to bomb the World Trade Center, but all that happened is that he had a gun that malfunctioned," the general said.

"Enough," the president said. "What do you mean, malfunctioned? I can't remember the details."

"Mulhaney lent his gun to someone who expressed an interest in buying it. The buyer took the gun to a gun range and shot it, and the gun went full auto. He took it back to Mulhaney, and Mulhaney was going to get it fixed, but before he could, the BATF showed up in the middle of the night and terrorized his family, put Mulhaney and his wife in the hospital, and destroyed his house," General Buchanan said.

"You forgot," the BATF director said, "that the team also recovered the machine gun."

"For Christ's sake, they recovered a malfunctioning AR-15."

"Gentlemen," the president interrupted, What does this have to do with old men shooting federal agents?"

"The old men who started this whole thing said that they'd served in World War II and that this BATF raid was just like stuff they had seen Hitler do in Germany," the Attorney General said. "At the memorial service for Aaron Silverman, the old man who was gunned down by the BATF, the surviving old men said that they saw the government of this country becoming oppressive."

"That's ridiculous," the Treasury Secretary said.

"Mr. President," the Attorney General said. "I think it would be well to consider that in these people's minds, the attacks were provoked."

"What difference does that make? You don't go around killing people who provoke you," the president said.

"Mr. President," the director of BATF said. "If people can shoot federal officers whenever they are provoked, the breakdown in social order will be even more complete than it already is."

The president said," I think these people were deranged. Nobody bothered them. And yet they saw fit to take the law into their own hands and start killing federal agents."

"Mr. President," the general said, "With respect, Sir, the old men were not deranged. They saw—and I'll have to say I see—the BATF's use of paramilitary tactics, personnel and equipment against civilians as a move toward a dictatorship. It wasn't about their guns, Sir, it was about tyrannical behavior of the government."

"I resent that, General," the BATF director said.

"I've heard enough, gentlemen. Uncontrolled lawlessness is not a legitimate form of protest against perceived wrongs committed by the government and I want it brought under control. What I'd like to know is why it would not be a good idea to issue an executive order banning the possession of all firearms."

There was a prolonged silence in the room.

"Mr. President, the General finally said, "I urge you to reconsider this, Sir. Such an executive order would be an over-reaction. We have a small problem caused by a renegade federal agency and three old men. That is not the kind of situation that could justify this type of executive order."

The BATF director stood and said, "We are not a renegade federal agency."

The Attorney General said, "I agree with the general, Mr. President, we can address this problem with a much less draconian approach."

"I don't see anything draconian about this approach," Fuller said. "Outlaws are killing federal agents with guns and so we ban guns. What's wrong with that"

"The Second Amendment , for one thing, has been held to protect the individual ownership of firearms," the Attorney General said.

"Well, I'm sure that makes sense when things are going well and federal agents aren't being gunned down by crazy men," the president said. "But surely that ruling would not apply in these circumstances."

"With respect, Sir, that's not the way it works. Constitutional rights do not depend on whether things go well or badly. They remain in effect even when things are going badly, and they apply especially in these circumstances," the Attorney General said.

The president said. "I have made it clear over and over, gentlemen, that I do not favor the civilian ownership of weapons.

"Mr. President, If you order the confiscation of all firearms, Sir, it is my duty to tell you that you will not only be breaking the law, but also you may be risking a civil war," the general said.

"Nonsense, General. This whole gun madness is an anachronism. No other civilized country allows its citizens to possess guns, and there's no reason we should be any different. Probably within our lifetimes, this country, Canada and Mexico will have merged into one country, and I can assure you that when that happens, there will be no private ownership of guns. So what I am doing only anticipates that."

"Mr. President," the Attorney General said, "As your chief law enforcement officer, I am telling you that you have no authority to confiscate guns owned by citizens. I don't know how else to say it."

"Mr. Attorney General, this is politics, not law, and as I have pointed out, the politics of this situation, the disappearance of borders to our north and south, within a few years, is going to result in the end of private citizens owning guns. But even if that were not the case, this situation demonstrates the folly of having private people own guns: they can turn them against the government."

"Sir", the general said, "at least for now, we still have borders in the north and south, and in any event, these weapons have been in the hands of citizens for two hundred years. It was only when this thug and his black suits started invading homes that they were turned against the government.

The director of BATF was again on his feet and the general looked like he was ready to come across the table at him.

The Attorney General held the director of BATF back and one of the general's aides restrained him from going over the conference table.

24

Thurmond Fuller was a politician's politician. He came from a poor family and went to school on scholarships available for low-income students. His mother, the only parent in the home, worked as a domestic. His father left when he was a small child, and Thurmond was close to his mother, who encouraged him to do well in school. Thurmond listened. He was near the top of his class in high school and was elected class president. Oddly, though Fuller was a sort of public figure in college, he had no close friends, and the few associates he did have were female, although he had no personal interest even in them. Following college, he received a Rhodes Scholarship to Oxford, where he studied international law. Upon returning to the States, he worked his way through George Washington University Law School in Washington, D.C.

Upon returning home to Findlay, Ohio, where he grew up, he ran successfully for city councilman, then mayor, and then for U.S. Congressman. He was a big frog in a small Ohio pond. A Rhodes Scholar. Although he was constantly presented by the local media as an eligible bachelor, Fuller had no lady friends. His life was politics and his passion was power. Nonetheless, Fuller's main constituency was women and younger voters, who were attracted to what the press called his progressivism. Fuller's main constituency was women and younger voters, who were attracted to what the press called his progressivism.

Among his colleagues, however, Fuller was described as shallow. He had a flair for dazzling crowds of people, but in committee rooms, where the work was done, he had nothing to contribute beyond the most banal of ideas. Because of this, it was generally agreed that Fuller would go far. If the Peter principle were not already in existence, it would have been invented for Fuller.

The big-money financial interests of the party, always on the look-out for a vehicle to represent them in public office, backed Fuller for U. S. Representative. With their backing, he won.

Fuller was an ideal vehicle for the interests of big money. He was not bright; he looked and sounded good; and the agents of big money could exploit his interest in power and high office. By the end of Fuller's first year in the House of Representatives, the courtship of Fuller by the large financial interests was in full swing, and they had begun to introduce him to the idea of a single government for all of North America. The reasons given were humanitarian-a higher standard of living for everyone-and the actual reasons-greater profits-remained unspoken. NAFTA and the exportation of jobs overseas was already a reality. Big money was only giving him a heads-up on what was inevitable.

After six years of indoctrination disguised as friendly consulations while Fuller was in the House of Representatives, the financial interests behind the party's power elite put Fuller forward as their candidate for president, and, after record spending to promote his candidacy, Fuller won the election. Agents of the financial interests had been at Fuller's side throughout the campaign, and when he took office, they remained near at hand. At first, Fuller was miffed by their insertion of themselves into his presidency, but within the first week, he realized that he needed them to get through the day. He was faced with one problem after another that he had no idea how to handle. The financial interests made sure that he had advisors to guide him through the difficulties.

After a time, it became obvious even to Fuller that the people who got him elected saw him as a tool. He was conflicted about this. On the one hand, it was o.k. to be a tool so long as they allowed him to sit on the throne. On the other hand, he didn't like being told what to do.

What Fuller needed, he realized, were some ideas of his own, something that neither the financial interests nor his staff could interfere with. He needed something in which he was the expert. One thing he was expert in was reading the minds of his female constituency. Fuller wasn't really very good at understanding how men thought. He had not grown up in the company of men, and his only real frame of reference was how women like his mother or his female friends saw the world.

There were, of course, a number of issues that concerned women voters, but many of them were counter-productive for him. On the issue of abortion, for example, there seemed to be as many women on one side as the other. Abortion was out. On the issue of the glass ceiling, there was potentially trouble with big corporate contributors if he championed women breaking through. That was out. But on the issue of gun ownership, although there were a number of women who owned and carried guns for defense, they were in the distinct minority. Gun ownership would be his issue. He would make the world safe for women and children. He would oppose the private ownership of guns.

Fuller's handlers loved it. They had been looking for ways to make Fuller seem like less of a tool, and this interest in banning guns would give him an identity and would mask their influence. He would seem to be a president who had ideas of his own. Not only that, but the whole gun issue was a potential stumbling block for the borderless North America that they had been working to realize.

Of course, Fuller knew that there was a Second Amendment and he knew that it had been interpreted by the United States Supreme Court in the Heller case to favor individual gun ownership rights, but what he was doing, he told himself, was politics, not law. He would oppose private gun ownership and win not only the female vote, but also the approbation of his financial party-elite. His staff could complain all they wanted, but this would be the area where he would tell them what to do and how to do it.

25

Three days after the cabinet meeting, President Thurmond Fuller executed his executive order banning the possession of firearms. There was, however, a grace period. The ban on possession of firearms was to go into effect two weeks after it was announced. During the two weeks, people could turn in their guns without penalty.

The executive order also suspended the requirements of the Fourth Amendment with respect to searches for and seizures of guns. Once the ban was in effect, police and military forces were authorized to enter homes, businesses, and any public or private dwelling for the purpose of seizing firearms.

There was, predictably, an outcry among pro-gun groups that the oppressor had finally identified himself, and vociferous speeches from liberals defending Fuller. The elimination of guns, they asserted, was long overdue. The country seemed poised on the brink of a civil war. Gun owners vowed to never give up their guns, and law enforcement agencies vowed that they would uphold the law.

But it was uncertain what the law was. On the face of it, the executive order seemed to violate the Second Amendment and the landmark Heller case, in which the United States Supreme Court held that citizens had the constitutional right to keep and bear arms. In fact, this argument was so compelling that large groups of citizens banded together to fund lawsuits challenging the executive order. The ACLU was among the plaintiffs in these suits. More than six hundred suits were filed in federal and state courts across the nation.

Meanwhile Jesse Washington and Jamie Berenger had moved into a safe house, which Sam and Nick maintained in the Bloomfield section of Pittsburgh. There was a nationwide APB for the two old men, but Sam and

Nick had spirited them away from Heinz Field before police could get organized to intercept them. They had entered the safe house through an underground garage seated in the back of a Land Cruiser with dark windows. No one knew they where they were.

When they got out of the truck and were led into the house, the old men were amazed to find themselves in a luxurious living space with hardwood floors, Persian rugs, comfortable furniture, books, and classical music in the background. They were also amazed to be greeted by Ronin, the hundred fifty pound Akita, who treated them like long lost members of his pack. He wagged his tail excessively, wagging his whole body, really, and gently grasped each of their wrists in his mouth, growling in a friendly way as he introduced them to dog greetings. Both men instantly fell in love with the big dog, and as he went back and forth between them for petting, their tension and their grief relaxed, giving way to smiles and caresses for the oversized canine.

After the old men got settled in, Sam fixed a gourmet salad with heavy buttered bread, and Nick warmed up noodle soup from Whole Foods. After they had eaten and had a second glass of red wine, both Jesse and Jamie announced they were ready for bed. Nick led them both upstairs to their rooms, and Ronin lay down in the hall midway between their doors.

In the days that followed, Jesse and Jamie began to show the effects of the strain they were under. Their friend was dead, they were fugitives, they had killed people, and they had taken on the whole United States government. On the second day, Nick engaged the old men in conversation at lunch.

Nick said, "How are you guys holding up? What do you think is going to come of all this?"

Jessie said, "Only one thing can happen now. BATF goes down the tubes and that fuckin president resigns."

"That's a big order," Sam said.

"We got no choice," Jamie Berenger said. "BATF killed Aaron and that president supported them. They both got to go."

"If they don't?" Nick said.

"That's fine. We'll kill 'em," Jesse said. "Or they'll kill us. Either way, we done what we could. We not gonna let that president play Hitler and we not gonna let the BATF be the SS."

"How do you propose to bring this off?" Sam said.

"What we always said," Jesse said. "We go on the internet and we tell the people that what we done so far isn't enough. We're now at war. It's time for them to start killing."

* * *

A week after the old men arrived at the safe house, Naratova called Sam, concerned about what the old men were going to do when the gun ban went into effect.

"Listen, Sam," Naratova said into the phone, "I'm counting on you to keep the lid on this thing as much as possible and I've got a related assignment for you."

"I don't like the sound of this," Sam said.

"Relax. It's not bad. Our intelligence is that there is opposition within the cabinet to this gun ban. We want to capitalize on that and we need you to do it."

"I'm an operator, Naratova, not a diplomat."

"I know that, Sam, but you're the only one who has contact with the old men, and the old men are key to keeping a lid on things."

"What do you want me to do?"

"I want you to meet with the Attorney General and some other members of the cabinet, maybe members of Congress, to figure out how to keep the country from lapsing into civil war."

"The only thing I've got to tell them is the old men want the president to resign and the BATF to be dissolved."

"Then tell them that."

"Are you serious?"

"Absolutely. You may be surprised to find how little disagreement there is between you."

* * *

Two days later, Sam walked into the Justice Department in Washington, D.C.

When he arrived at the Attorney General's office, an aide escorted him in immediately. The tenth floor office had a magnificent view of the Washington Mall through windows that must have been ten feet tall. In front of the windows sat the Attorney General, behind a desk cluttered with files, photographs, and books.

In front of the desk was a magnificent deep blue-purple silk Tabriz, and arranged in a semi-circle on the Tabriz were six overstuffed armchairs. Three of them were occupied, and the occupants stood when Sam was brought into the room.

The aide took Sam directly down the middle aisle through the chairs and introduced him to Sean Carnegie, the Attorney General. The aide then turned and introduced Sam to the other men, Rutherford Mason, Speaker of the House, Colonel James Mansfield, aide to General Buchanan, who was unable to be present, and Henry Beauchamp, Director of Homeland Security.

The Attorney General began. "We understand that you have worked for many years with the CIA, Mr. Budda, that you are highly regarded, and that you are also somehow involved with the old men who started this malay."

"Yes, sir. My partner and I operate a personal protection agency and Aaron--the old man who was killed by the BATF in the park-contacted me and asked me to be his messenger to the BATF. I agreed, and I took his message to the head of the Pittsburgh office of BATF."

"What was the message?" Carnegie said.

"It was that if the BATF would release Clyde Mulhaney and stop invading people's home with thugs, the client would not kill any ATF agents," Sam said.

"Oh yeah," Carnegie said. "That's the letter that was published in the newspaper isn't it?"

"Yes," Sam said.

"So you met with BATF and them told them what the demands were?" Beauchamp said.

"Yes."

"And their response?" Carnegie said.

"They arrested me, wired my house to record the client when he called next, and threatened me and my client with various unpleasant outcomes."

"They weren't interested in what you had to say?" Colonel Mansfield said.

"No," Sam said. "They were mostly interested in impressing me with how tough they are and how my client was going to jail."

"What was your client's reaction?" the Attorney General said.

"He called my house to ask about my meeting with BATF. I was in jail when he called, and some BATF agent answered. The client demanded to speak with me, so they let me out of the lockup, and he told them through me that he was sending a letter to the Post Gazette and if they did not see that it was published, he would start killing BATF agents."

"They ignored him, I assume," Beauchamp said.

"Yes. But remember, although I only knew about Aaron , there were three of them all along, Aaron , Jamie Berenger and Jesse Washington. I thought I had one client, but three men were involved."

"O.K.," Beauchamp said, "Basically, the BATF blew off the threat."

"Yes."

"Why did these guys insist on going through you? Why not just talk to the BATF themselves?" Beauchamp said.

"I asked the caller that myself. He said that he wanted an outside person to know what he had told BATF so that they would not be able to lie about it," Sam said.

"Are these guys really eighty years old?" Colonel Mansfield said.

"Yes, sir. They are."

"What happened then?" Mason said.

"After they killed the first agent, once again they gave BATF a chance to understand they weren't bluffing and to talk about their demands. But BATF just stonewalled, and that's when the old men shot the guy who ran the Pittsburgh ATF office."

"Did ATF want to talk after that?" Carnegie said.

"Well, they said they did want to talk. They offered Aaron immunity if he would come in. But I'm getting ahead of myself. Let me go back. After the old men shot the head of the Pittsburgh Office of ATF, Nick and I started looking for them."

"Any luck?" Carnegie said.

"Yeah. We found them and we talked to them," Sam said.

"You didn't turn them in?" Beauchamp said.

"They were our clients," Sam said.

"How did you find them when police forces all over the country have failed?" Mason said.

"We studied the second shooting and worked off clues in that shooting," Sam said.

"All right, you found them. What happened then?" Beauchamp said.

"At the clients' request, I contacted BATF again and asked whether they were going to meet the clients' demands. They said that they would meet the demands and give the client immunity if he gave himself up," Sam said.

"Is that how they got him? He gave himself up?" Colonel Mansfield said. "Yes."

"I thought the BATF said they found this guy through superior police work," Carnegie said. "I thought that's what all the hoopla was about when the Director of ATF went to Pittsburgh to give everybody medals."

"Well," Sam said. "Let's just say the BATF was a little less than honest in its description of how they got Aaron."

"So Aaron surrendered because they were going to give him immunity?"

"Yes. I went with him and they arrested us both and knocked us around a bit."

"How did you get out?" Colonel Mansfield said.

"Greggory Naratova, of the CIA, put a word in for me."

"Why would the CIA want to get involved in a high profile thing like this?" Mason asked.

"The CIA had contacted me early on because the threats to BATF were happening in Pittsburgh and I was in Pittsburgh. They were concerned about the possibility of civil war. It was just an accident that the guys they were concerned about were my clients. When the CIA found this out, they said that if I would try to keep a lid on this and keep them informed, they would bail me out if I needed it."

"Interesting," Beauchamp said. "What happened then?"

"Then Aaron was released by the federal court because the government's case was defective, and we got Aaron away from the federal court before they could re-arrest him with a new warrant. We also set up a rally for him at a city park. More than ten thousand people showed up, and then the federal agents showed up too with an arrest warrant for Aaron. They were going to re-arrest him."

"Why did you want to have him appear in front of a huge crowd," Beauchamp asked.

"I wanted the crowd to have a leader, someone they could trust, and ultimately, someone who could keep them in check," Sam said.

"But he didn't get to become the leader," Carnegie said.

"No. The federal agents plowed into the crowd with their cars and trucks, but they got bogged down about halfway up the hill where Aaron was, and then they got out and forced their way up the hill. But before they got to the top, they started shooting into the crowd. The crowd tried to run away. Some of them made it and some did not. When the BATF got close to Aaron, he was surrounded by a circle of men who were protecting him, and the BATF just shot him. Then they arrested all the men who were around him."

"Did you get arrested?" Beauchamp said.

"Yes. Both Nick and I. Once again, Naratova got us out."

"So where are we now?" Carnegie said.

"The bad news is that the president has made things worse by his executive order that bans the possession of guns. The good news is that Aaron's buddies, Jamie Berenger and Jesse Washington have become the leaders. They appeared at Aaron's memorial service and they are the only hope we have of keeping this thing from spiraling out of control," Sam said.

"Naratova was right about you," Carnegie said. "He said we'd be glad we had you on board."

"Thank you, sir," Sam said. "I'm not comfortable in this role of political activist. I tend to be more in the shadows."

"You're doing fine, Mr. Budda," Mason said. "Take it from an old politician. We need you on this. You have abilities and contacts that we don't have. And we can work together."

"Thank you, sir," Sam said. "I certainly agree with you that we need each other to win this thing, and I will do my best to hold up my end."

"So how do we work together to keep this from spiraling out of control, as you put it," Colonel Mansfield said.

"You aren't going to like this," Sam said. "There's only one way. The president has to resign and the BATF has to be dissolved."

There was silence in the room for a full minute.

"Why do you say that, Sam?" Carnegie said.

"Because that's what Jamie Berenger and Jesse say, and they won't be argued with. Remember, Aaron was their buddy and these guys killed him," Sam said.

"Can't you reason with them?" Beauchamp said. "What they want would be very difficult."

"Here's the thing, Mr. Beauchamp. If the president doesn't resign and this executive order goes into effect, Jesse and Jamie Berenger will go on the internet, and you'll have a civil war of a kind that will rip the country to shreds. There are at least 500,000 guys out there with high-powered rifles who will start using them. And you'll never be able to stop it because they'll be ordinary citizens who will kill one agent a week and then go home to meat and potatoes just like nothing had happened," Sam said, "And after a while, others will be emboldened, and more agents will die. Of course, at some point, the government will pull out all of the stops by imposing a police state, and full fledged civil war will be in effect."

Carnegie said, "Beauchamp, do you think that is possible?"

"I think it is more than possible. It is likely," Beauchamp said. "There is a very strong minority in this country who will not be disarmed, and they will die resisting it. If they acted as individuals, we could defeat them. But if they act as a group directed by these old men and use the strategy of shooting and then fading into the woodwork, they would be almost impossible to defeat."

"Jesus," Mason said.

"I told you, you wouldn't like it," Sam said. "But don't forget the positive part. If it weren't for Jesse and Jamie Berenger, we would have absolutely no way to control the public response to the executive order and the BATF."

"So how do you propose we use them?" Buchanan said.

"It's simple," Sam said. "Your part is to get the president to resign and to abolish the BATF. My part is to get Jamie Berenger and Jesse to tell people to go home and cool off without shooting up the government after the president is gone."

"Is that all?" Mason said, chuckling.

"Admittedly, Rutherford, what Sam is suggesting is extreme, but the bottom line is that the president has moved the country toward a civil war, and that is an impeachable offense," the Attorney General said. "I think you could even make a case for treason."

There was a murmur of assent.

"Am I to assume then, gentlemen, that we are on the same page and that we will work together to get this president out of office and to keep people from going berserk?" Sam said.

"Yes. I think you can assume that, Sam," Beauchamp said.

"I think it's safe to say we are on the same page Sam," Carnegie said, getting up to escort Sam out of the office. "We politicians need to meet now to figure out how to do our part of things."

"You have a number for me. Let me know if you need anything. I think we are all aware that time is a problem. Jesse and Jamie Berenger have told me that they will go on the internet right before the gun ban goes into effect. After that, the shooting will start and we will have to try to figure out how to stop it."

Sam left the meeting and flew back to Pittsburgh, satisfied he finally had some allies in the government who might be able to avert disaster.

The Colonel, the Attorney General, the Speaker of the House, and the Secretary of Homeland Security also were pleased to think that they had an inside voice in the gun owners' camp. When Sam had gone, they discussed what needed to be done.

Colonel Mansfield said, "The entire Joint Chiefs of Staff is with General Buchanan on this, gentlemen. The General will now meet with each of the Chiefs individually and tell them that we intend to remove the president so they are not blind-sided and will have some idea of what to do in the event he gives a crazy order, like declaring martial law and suspending all civil rights."

"Excellent, Colonel," Carnegie said. "How about you, Mr. Speaker?"

Mason said, "I have already begun work on an impeachment document. I had no idea I'd have this much support from other branches of government, but that will make it that much easier."

"Mr. Beauchamp?" Carnegie said.

"I'll begin talks with the other law enforcement agencies, particularly the FBI and the various state agencies that are related to us, counseling a cooling down of this gun thing," he said.

"For my part," Carnegie said, "I will be talking with the various U.S. Attorneys and state Attorney Generals. I will order the federal people to offer no cooperation in prosecuting anyone arrested for a gun crime and to discourage any police work in that direction. I control the FBi and there will be no FBI involvement."

The meeting broke up with each of the four men feeling a sense of hope that was absent when their meeting began.

26

As the days went on, it became widely known that there was a movement within the government to remove the president from office. Secretly, the Attorney General met with the Secretaries of Commerce, the Interior, Labor, Veteran's Affairs, and State. They shared his concerns and supported the movement to remove Thurmond Fuller from office. The Secretaries of Housing and Urban Development, Education, and the Treasury supported the president.

By the end of the first week, the president was aware that there was significant resistance in the government to the executive order, and he asked for information from his cabinet on this resistance. Several cabinet members suggested that the opposition to this executive order was so significant that there was apparently a movement to impeach the president. The Attorney General urged the president to save himself from this conflict.

The beginning of the second week of the hiatus, the House was openly debating articles of impeachment, and Speaker Mason came to the president with a delegation from both houses of Congress to ask that that the president reconsider his decision to implement the gun ban.

Schoefield Brown, the ranking member of the Senate who came with the delegation, who was widely thought of as the grand old man of the Senate, began the meeting. "Mr. President, as you can see from the membership of this group, there is bipartisan concern about your decision to ban guns by executive order."

"What is the concern, Mr. Brown?" the president said.

"There are a number of concerns, but I'll trouble you with only two. First, we are convinced that banning the possession of firearms is unconstitutional. Second, if it is constitutional, it seems to us that it should be the business of the Congress, not of the executive, to put it into effect," Brown said.

"But the Congress has not acted, Mr. Brown," the president said.

"Mr. President, with respect, the Congress does not dictate a timetable for your actions, and you should not expect to be able to dictate a timetable for ours."

"It's not a question of timetables, Mr. Brown," the president said. "It's a question of the Congress's willingness to act. When I put the executive order into effect, the matter was not even up for debate in Congress. If I waited for the Congress to act, I sincerely believe that I would wait forever."

"If that is the case, Mr. President, that is the prerogative of the Congress," Brown said.

"Mr. President," the Speaker of the House said, "I urge you to consider that if you proceed with this executive order, you will have placed the country in a constitutional crisis. Not only is the viability of the gun ban at issue under the Second Amendment, but also, you yourself may be impeached."

"Mr. Mason," the president said, "if the country is placed in jeopardy, it will be you gentlemen, not I, who has done it. I am acting to preserve the peace and tranquility of the nation, and you gentlemen don't have the good sense to see it."

"Mr. President," Mason began . . .

"Gentlemen," the president said, "thank you for coming. This meeting is over"

The Congressional delegation returned to the Capital, miffed and determined to bring the debate on the impeachment of Thurmond Fuller to a quick conclusion.

Later that day, the Chairman of the Joint Chiefs phoned the president and told him that in every military installation across the country, there was concern among commanders that soldiers might refuse the order to seize guns from civilians and to use deadly force if necessary while doing it.

The director of the FBI also told the president that police chiefs in every major city were concerned about the willingness of their officers to carry out the gun ban and about armed resistance by citizens.

The Secretary of Homeland Security phoned the president that he was concerned about sabotage of critical governmental services if the executive order were implemented.

In a brief meeting with the Attorney General and the Secretary of Homeland Security, the president disregarded Carnegie's concern that legal challenges to this executive order had been filed in every federal and state court in the nation. He also disregarded Beauchamp's concern that implementing the executive order might involve the significant disruption of public services and it might cause the Congress to speed up its impeachment proceedings.

"Gentlemen," he said, "I will not be dissuaded."

27

Two days before the executive order was to be implemented, newspapers across the nation carried the front-page story that the gun ban would go into effect on Monday.

Sam, Nick and the old men were having breakfast at the safe house and reading newspapers from around the state.

"Looks like your people in Washington weren't too persuasive," Jamie Berenger said, drinking his coffee.

"I guess not," Sam said.

"We go online tomorrow," Jesse said.

"I know," Sam said, "We've done what we can do."

"Do you think we're right, Sam?" Jamie Berenger said.

"Yes. If the government takes everyone's guns, there will be no hope of resisting a runaway government."

"Some people don't think the government will ever become a dictator," Jesse said.

Nick said, "I'm always impressed by the stories about the last days of Nixon's presidency. Remember? It was during the time the Watergate scandal was being investigated and the White House had been ordered to turn over certain tapes to the federal district court. Apparently Schlesinger, the Secretary of Defense, and the Pentagon were afraid President Nixon would crack up and order federal troops to defend the White House against US Marshals. They were afraid Nixon would precipitate a constitutional melt-down."

"Good example, Nick," Sam said. "The people who think the government will never run amok don't know anything about government. Government is just made up of people, and people sometimes go nuts. In fact, that's what's happening right now. This executive order is the act of a madman."

Nick said, "I've heard it said that being in the White House makes everyone crazy. It's just a matter of how long it takes."

Sunday afternoon, Jesse posted their message on the internet, and within the hour, it had been viewed by more than a million people. The message read:

> *Brothers and Sisters,*
>
> *We hoped this day would never come, but it has. The president has announced that two days from now, none of us can possess a gun. When that happens, we will have no way to defend ourselves from crime or the government.*
>
> *The government has already killed Aaron and a hundred other people who came to the rally to hear what Aaron had to say. The government has already invaded Clyde Mulhaney's home with combat troops, all because his rifle misfired. We fear the government. Aaron used to say that if his people in Poland had guns when Hitler tried to put them on the trains, maybe so many would not have died. Or maybe they would, but at least they would have done their best to stay alive. That is all we want to do.*
>
> *Here's what we propose. When they come for the guns, kill them. Otherwise, they will kill you. They have orders to use deadly force and to invade your homes without warrants. If they don't kill you before they get your guns, they'll kill you after, because then you'll be an easy target, just like Aaron's people in Europe.*
>
> *And when you get through killing the police who come for the guns, turn your attention to the BATF. Listed below are the names of every BATF agent in the United States, with their addresses and social security numbers. Look them up and kill them. Or if you're good with a computer and you don't want to shoot them, take their social security numbers and ruin their credit and their reputations.*
>
> *The government says that this is about guns. It isn't. It is about the freedom of ordinary people. It is about people who don't even own guns. Those who don't own guns benefit from those who do. So long as there are gun owners, the government will be hesitant to run over the rights of ordinary people. When the gun owners are gone, the rest of you will just be so many Jews lined up at the railroad station.*
>
> *A final message to the police and the military men who are asked to carry out the gun ban. You know it's wrong to seize our*

guns and you know it's wrong to act against your fellow citizens who are not criminals. So don't do it. Resign. You are not our enemy, but if you come for our guns, you will become our enemy. Come back to this web site every day for follow-ups.

Jesse Washington
Jamie Berenger

What followed then were a hundred pages of names and addresses of BATF agents.

28

There were two major headlines in Monday's Pittsburgh Post Gazette. On the top left was the headline, "ARTICLES OF IMPEACHMENT ARE FILED AGAINST PRESIDENT." On the top right was the headline "POLICE GEAR UP FOR GUN GRAB."

The impeachment story quoted Rutherford Mason, Speaker of the House, who said that the articles of impeachment had been drawn up and served on the president, and that pending negotiations between the leadership of the House and Senate, a trial would be scheduled as soon as possible. He explained further that the articles of impeachment were based on the charge that the president had needlessly and illegally risked plunging the nation into a civil war over the gun issue. He stated that he was not himself in favor of citizens owning assault weapons, but that it was an impeachable offense to risk a civil war to achieve that goal.

The gun story described the internet posting of Jesse and Jamie Berenger. It also reported that police had drawn up lists of those who owned guns but had not turned them in during the amnesty period. These lists were based on computer files of gun ownership which police departments across the country had kept, often illegally. The plan was to invade the homes of those whose files indicated they had the largest number of guns.

The story also reported that police SWAT teams had been chosen as the logical instrumentalities to carry out these raids. They were heavily armored, mobile, fearsome, and trained in close quarters combat. Finally, it reported that police were authorized to use deadly force against those who resisted.

* * *

On Monday morning, the gun ban was in effect across the nation. In every major city, black trucks stood by while battle-dressed SWAT teams loaded up the gear they would use to deal with recalcitrant gun owners who had not given up their guns during the amnesty period. By mid-morning on Monday, however, news leaked out that the gun operations had been somewhat delayed by the fact that in one large city after another, significant numbers of SWAT team members called off sick. The teams were finally deployed, but none of them got through the day without bloodshed.

In Indianapolis, the SWAT command had identified J.J. Beardsley as a large owner-collector of firearms. Their records indicated that Beardsley owned almost two hundred rifles, pistols, and shotguns, and he had turned in none of them during the amnesty. The team waited until Beardsley and his wife left for work, and then moved in with their newly purchased "door buster." It was a gasoline powered hydraulic mechanism that ripped doors from the jams. As three of the SWAT team members were firing up the door buster and positioning its arms on the front door, all three were shot and killed with high-powered rifle fire coming through the door.

Other team members, who had been lounging on the lawn and leaning against trees also came under fire and two more were immediately wounded, again with high powered rifle fire. The SWAT team immediately deployed to defensive positions and called for backup. Steady fire came from various windows of the house and two more SWAT team members were shot dead. Now a massive amount of fire was poured into the house, almost blindly. One trooper, firing an H&K .308 battle rifle, emptied several twenty round magazines into all parts of the house. A number of these rounds penetrated the house and also the walls of a nearby house, killing a 35-year-old housewife who was feeding her infant child breakfast next door.

The pitched gun battle went on for almost two more hours, taking the lives of three more SWAT troopers. The occupants of the house seemed to have an uncanny ability to move from one window to the next, apparently firing from behind barricaded positions, and often firing simultaneously from three separate parts of the house, and even vents in the roof. When gas was finally shot into the house and no one came out, commandos entered and found the bodies of three boys, aged 13, 15 and 16. One was the son of the homeowner and others were his friends. The body of the housewife was not discovered until her husband came home in the early afternoon because he was unable to raise her on the phone.

In Idaho, a gun owner who had planted explosive charges around his house blew up his home, himself and most of the yard, including a twenty-member SWAT team when they surrounded his house.

In Pennsylvania, a gun owner living on a farm used a .50 caliber rifle to hold off a SWAT team, firing from a barricaded hillside, which he had prepared in anticipation of the assault. The gun owner and thirteen policemen were killed before the incident was ended.

In Florida, gun owners who lived close to each other surrounded a SWAT team, which had approached the house of one of their number. Using .30 caliber rifles, the gun owners killed the entire team of twenty-two.

In New Mexico, a street gang followed a SWAT team for an entire day and then at the end of the day, attacked the SWAT truck with automatic weapons. All fifteen SWAT team members were killed as they sat inside the SWAT truck, which was riddled with as many as five hundred bullet holes. The gang also captured the van following the truck, which was loaded with hundreds of confiscated guns.

In West Virginia, a caravan of twenty-two police vehicles was stopped on a winding back road surrounded on both sides by steep hills. The convoy was en route to the home of a wealthy gun collector. They were stopped by boulders, which blocked the road after they had been dynamited from the hills towering above the road. When the police cars attempted to turn around, more boulders and trees were dynamited onto the road at the end of the convoy, and the trapped policemen were gunned down by an unknown number of men armed with high powered hunting rifles shooting from the hills above them. Forty-seven officers died, some of them in their cars, and some in the woods, where they were apparently trying to flee.

In Chicago, a gun owner had removed all of his guns from his house and had put them in the trunk of his car. He hoped to find a place to hide them and had decided to put them in a rented storage facility for the time being. He was on his way out of the driveway when a SWAT truck pulled up behind him and ordered him to stop. He sped away from the SWAT truck, and it followed him with red lights blazing and a loudspeaker demanding that he pull over. Four blocks later, he was stopped in gridlocked traffic in the midst of an apartment complex, and the SWAT truck caught up to him, ordering him out of the car on the loudspeaker. Black-suited SWAT troopers poured out of the truck and surrounded the car with their weapons pointed at the driver. He remained locked in the car and would not get out.

One of the troopers smashed the window on the driver's side with the butt of his rifle, and then slumped to the ground. He had been shot with a 7mm magnum round fired from an elevated position. The SWAT team was taking fire from the windows of the apartment complexes that surrounded the car. Within seconds, seven SWAT troopers fell to the ground, mortally wounded, and the rest ran for the cover of doorways and trees.

As soon as the gridlock cleared, the man in the car sped away, leaving the SWAT truck behind riddled with bullets. Dead and wounded SWAT team members lay scattered over the area. Subsequent police raids on the apartment complex turned up nothing.

In Ohio, a warehouse storing weapons seized over a five-day period by joint enforcement teams from Cuyahoga County was broken into and several thousand confiscated guns were stolen. Three private police guards were handcuffed and executed.

In Maine, a state police barracks was attacked by gunmen using semi-automatic assault weapons. Seven state policemen were killed, all of the weapons secured in the barracks were taken, and the barracks and the cars parked there were burned.

In Virginia, thieves disguised as police went door-to-door demanding that people turn over their guns. They had collected an unknown number of weapons over a four-hour period, when a suspicious neighbor called 911. The two officers who responded were killed by automatic weapons fire and the assailants escaped.

In Tennessee, a local police station at which a SWAT team was based was leveled by an explosion caused by a rented truck parked outside containing a fertilizer bomb. Eighteen people died when the bomb ignited, destroying the police station and catching fire to homes and businesses nearby. Numerous others besides the eighteen dead were hospitalized with injuries.

In Maryland, police surprised a large group of neighbors who were burying weapons in sealed containers in a wooded section of a city park. In the gun battle that ensued, twelve officers and four civilians were killed.

In all, seven hundred incidents of clashes with police were reported on the first day of the implementation of the president's order.

By the fifth day of implementation, more than three thousand incidents of citizens clashing with police over the seizure of guns were reported, and law enforcement agencies in every part of the country were expressing concerns.

29

The president was now convening emergency cabinet meetings every day to discuss the problems that were being encountered in implementing the gun ban. On the second day, the meeting was opened by a report from the Chairman of the Joint Chiefs.

"Mr. President," the Chairman of the Joint Chiefs of Staff began, "we have reports of mutiny at every major military installation where the troops have been ordered to participate in the gun confiscation program. In most locations, the mutiny has taken the form of refusal to follow orders to participate in the confiscation. Several hundred soldiers are in the brigs. In two locations, one in Wisconsin and one in Idaho, troops have openly rebelled and have set up defensive positions, which have been, of course, surrounded by loyal troops and light armor."

After a silence in the room, the director of BATF said, "Why don't you just shoot them for failing to follow orders?"

The general, who had seemed strained while presenting his material, got red in the face and said, "Mr. President, I do not suffer fools gladly, and unless you order me to answer this man, I will ignore him."

Again, silence. Then the president said, "Please answer his question, General."

"Sir, it will do us no good to win the battle and lose the war. Right now we do not know how many other soldiers are thinking about mutiny. We have to assume that those who have mutinied have friends who have not, but who might change their minds if they perceive that their friends are being shot for following their conscience. We are trying to contain the mutiny, not exacerbate it. You have to understand that the idea of confiscating guns is not popular in the armed services. Soldiers imagine that they might be deployed to forcefully take guns from their fathers or their brothers."

"Sounds to me like you don't have control of the troops," the director of BATF said.

The general turned, furious, to the director and said, "It is because of your stupidity that we face this situation. The problem is not my control and it is not my troops. It is your wanting to play Rambo with civilians. Why don't you try coming to my house at four in the morning, Mr. Director?"

"Gentlemen, that's enough," the president said. Mr. Attorney General, what's the situation with state and local police forces?"

"Pretty much the same as with the military, Mr. President. In every major city, hundreds of cops called off sick on the day they were assigned to the gun confiscation details. On the other hand, there's been no outright rebellion or refusal to perform the confiscations."

"Any other problems?" the President asked.

"Yes, Sir," the Director of the FBI said. "Although most of the gun violence has been directed at police agencies who were trying to confiscate guns, we are now seeing an increase in the number of shootings of BATF agents and of other police officers who have had no part in the gun confiscations. This is apparently in response to the internet communications of the two old men who remain at large and who published the names of BATF agents and their addresses. So far a hundred seventeen fatal police shootings have been reported.

"In addition, across the country in all police agencies, unusually large numbers of officers have taken early retirement and there are still a large number of officers who have called off work sick."

"All right," the president said, anything else?"

"Yes sir," the Secretary of Homeland Security said, "Although it has not been reported on the news, we have discovered a number of crude explosive devices attached to power transformers, police stations, and bridge supports in various parts of the country. We have defeated all of these attempts by discovering them before they blew up, but that was only luck. As time goes on and these amateurs get more practice, they will get better at what they're doing, and we are going to have some explosions."

"That does it," the president fumed. "I have been patient and I have been consistent in showing that I would not be opposed in the implementation of this gun ban. But that was not sufficient. As of now, I am placing the nation's twenty-five largest cities under martial law, and the National Guard and the regular army are to enforce the martial law. Anything else, gentlemen?"

There was complete silence in room. The quiet sound of air circulating in the room seemed loud.

The headlines in the next day's Post Gazette were: PRESIDENT DECLARES MARTIAL LAW IN MAJOR CITIES." The sub-heading was: "Police, the National Guard, and Federal agencies are ordered to confiscate guns. The possession of assault rifles, handguns, and of all firearms is forbidden by executive order. Resistance is to be met with deadly force."

30

Later that day, Attorney General Carnegie convened a meeting in his office. Present were The Secretary of Homeland Security, Beauchamp, the Speaker of the House, Rutherford Mason, The Chairmen of the Joint Chiefs, General Buchanan, and Sam Budda.

After everyone had been introduced, Carnegie summarized the most recent cabinet meeting in which the president had declared martial law. Then, because Sam and General Buchanan had not met before, Carnegie introduced them and explained that Sam was their link with the rebels.

"Sam is here, General Buchanan, because he is affiliated with the old men who are so famous now as gun rights protesters."

"I see," the general said. "What kind of affiliation do you have with these old men?"

"I represent them in dealing with the government."

"Are you their lawyer?"

"No. I'm an ex-CIA operative. These old men looked me up for some reason to carry their demands to the BATF, and when the CIA found that out, they asked me to stay involved with the old men for the purpose of using them, if the opportunity presents, to keep a lid on things."

"And how do you propose to use them?" the general asked.

"Initially, the plan was to convince the government that could not win the gun ban issue without civil war, and it would back down. The old men would then communicate with the country at large through the internet and make the case for non-violence."

"So where are you now?" Carnegie said.

"Now, because of martial law and the gun ban, the old men are demanding the resignation of the president. I have a plan to get that done," Sam said.

"Please," Carnegie said, "go on."

"First of all, gentlemen, I assume we can agree time is not on our side. The longer martial law is in effect, the more shooting there will be."

"Agreed," they all said.

"That means we have to act expeditiously," Sam said. "Here is my plan. Tomorrow, in the middle of the night, people working with me, will begin to fire .50 caliber rifles into the White House. There will be a number of shooters, and we are planning to fire about four hundred rounds."

"Jesus Christ," Buchanan said.

The mood in the room changed. They reality of the situation was soaking in. Armed conflict. An attack on the White House. There was an uneasy shuffling in the chairs and a murmur of protest that this was outrageous.

"Hear me out," Sam said.

"The object is not to hit anyone, but if we do hit someone, that is just one of the costs of doing business. Following our attack, which will last for less than three minutes, predictably, some sort of state of emergency will be declared and the military will be called on for protection. Undoubtedly, the Secret Service will try to move the president out of the White House."

"You bet they will," Beauchamp said.

"Well, they won't be able to, because the general here will order the presidential helicopter to stand down, and in response to the emergency declared by the White House, he will send troops into the District to form a perimeter around the White House, and these troops will refuse to allow any cars in or out, including the presidential limousine."

"The Secret Service may start shooting if we do that," the general said.

"Not if they are looking down the barrels of several .50 caliber machine guns at every check point," Sam said.

"All right," Mason said. "He stays in the White House. Then what?"

"Then you, Mr. Mason, and your Congressional delegation go to him with a demand that he resign. You tell him that the votes have already been counted, and that he will be impeached. Not only that, but under the rules of this proceeding, the only question will be whether he imposed the gun ban. If he did, the verdict must be guilty. The trial will take five minutes. If he does not show up, he will be found guilty in absentia."

"Pretty impressive," Carnegie said. "I like it."

"Mr. Carnegie," Sam said, "am I right in thinking that at least one federal court has issued an injunction against enforcing the gun ban?"

"Yes. The D.C. Circuit and the Seventh Circuit have both issued preliminary injunctions, and four other circuits have cases scheduled within the next two days. The preliminary injunction means that the government cannot proceed until a hearing takes place and the court decides whether the injunction should be made permanent or dismissed."

"Good," Sam said. "This is where you come in, general. You surround the White House when the state of emergency is declared, and you pull all troops off enforcement of the gun ban. You issue an order that no troops are to be used to enforce martial law on the grounds that federal courts have put a hold on enforcement. You cannot honor the Executive Order, because it is, in effect, an illegal document until the courts approve it. And, of course, you will also have to order all presidential aircraft to remain on the ground."

"What else?" Mason said.

"You, Mr. Attorney General, will accompany Mr. Mason's group and offer the legal opinion that they are empowered to do what they say they will do. You should also point out that the president is not allowed to do what he is doing because of the federal court decisions."

"And what about me, Mr. Budda?" Beauchamp said.

"You, Mr. Beauchamp, will order a complete lockdown of all commercial flights in the United States, beginning with the implementation of the state of emergency. That will prevent any of Thurmond's friends from flying in to offer support. It will also seem a natural part of the state of emergency."

"And how does this all come together, Mr. Budda?" General Buchanan said.

"Fuller is being shot at in the White House; he's being impeached; he's being told that the federal courts are against him; he can't even fly out of the White House; and his generals refuse to obey his orders. He can't leave and he can't tell anybody what to do. If he stays, the Congress is going to prosecute him. That's when you gentlemen are nearby to help him sign the resignation papers."

"And if he refuses?" General Buchanan said.

"Then you convene an emergency session of the Congress and go through the impeachment proceedings," Sam said. "In the meantime, the gun confiscation is on hold because of the court injunctions and because the army is unwilling to defy the courts."

31

For the rest of that day and the next day the president stormed around the White House, barging into and out of aides' offices, asking questions and then leaving before they could be answered, and blowing up at anyone who crossed him. The reports coming in were that although martial law had been imposed in the major cities, police were being killed and shot at on an unprecedented scale. In Chicago, Philadelphia, Las Vegas, Denver, Atlanta, Detroit, Miami and Los Angeles, neighborhood police stations were barricaded with sandbags and were under attack. Homeland Security was reporting incidents of sabotage everywhere, and in Oregon, power had been knocked out for the entire state. Gun confiscation had come to almost a complete halt. Across the country, whenever teams started out, they came under heavy fire and had to turn back. Only military groups in heavily armoured columns had been able to get through.

The evening of the second day, the president was beside himself with anxiety, doubt and rage. No wonder he felt this way, he realized. His entire cabinet was of no help. Those who didn't oppose him didn't really support him. There was no way he could count on any of them. He was in this himself, except for that moron who ran the BATF, and with all the opposition he was getting, it was beginning to take its toll.

The Vice President, Jason Reynolds, had remained out of sight in this entire controversy. It was time he made an appearance. At least he could be supportive. Fuller's secretary called the Vice President about 10:00 p.m., and it took him almost an hour to get to the White House. He walked into the Oval Office at approximately 11:00 p.m.

"Hello Jason," the president said, standing to greet him.

"Mr. President," Reynolds said, advancing and shaking hands.

"Have a seat, Jason. You've been conspicuous by your absence," the president said.

"I decided to stay out of the way until you decided that I had some role to play," Reynolds said.

"Well, I need you in the role of supporter. The cabinet is useless. They either oppose me or sit on the fence waiting to see which way the bullet flies, as it were."

"You know I support you in this. It is time guns were removed as a fact of life in this country. Every civilized nation in the world except us has taken guns away from ordinary citizens. It's time we caught up."

"You have no idea how good it is to hear you speak common sense. I'm constantly having to deal with drivel about the Constitution and tyranny and the right of self-defense. I'm so sick of it I could puke."

"What can I do to help?" Reynolds said.

"I'm not sure, but from now on, I want you to attend the cabinet meetings and to move into that vacant office down the hall so that I will have you nearby. I just need some support. I get tired of all the opposition."

"Well, I'm not sure what the opposition . . . ."

Fuller had a sense of glass shattering and a loud thud, and simultaneously of being showered by thin shards of glass. He would later figure out the large window behind him had shattered when it was penetrated by a .50 caliber bullet that hit Reynolds in the chest as he sat facing the president. What Fuller saw was Reynolds's body exploding in a spray of blood as the impact of the bullet propelled his chair backwards, plowing furrows in the Persian rug until the chair and the dead Vice President crashed into an interior wall of the Oval Office.

As the president sat dumbfounded, immobilized and traumatized, gripping the edge of his massive desk, smoke from the burning body set off fire alarms and the stench of burned flesh filled the air. Two secret service agents ran into the room carrying submachine guns. They rushed toward the president, as sirens went off all over the White House complex. The agents grabbed the president under the arms and rushed him away from the bulletproof windows, which the .50 caliber bullet had easily penetrated, and into an inner hallway. The president lay on the floor covered by a flack jacket, with one agent crouched at his head and the other at his feet with their sub-machine guns covering the hall in both directions. The sirens continued to wail. The White House was in a complete lockdown.

Uniformed guards slipped into combat gear and deployed .30 caliber auto loading rifles. Plainclothes agents put on level 3 vests and brandished submachine guns. Communication was automatically switched to combat mode, with each battle group tied in to a commander, and the various commanders into the situation commander in the White House basement. Apart from battle group commanders, agents guarding the president also had direct access to the situation commander.

"CICUS is in the secure hall outside the Oval Office," the lead agent said into his headset. CICUS was an acronym for Commander in Chief United States.

"Stay put until CICUS group number 1 gets there," the situation commander said.

Within seconds, a group of five plainclothes agents wearing battle vests hastily donned over their suits, ran into the secure hallway and rushed the president down the hall to a double locked emergency door leading to the basements. The president was taken down three levels, passing various secure doors and guards, until he got to the situation room. He arrived breathless and shaken.

"My wife . . . " he said.

"She's safe, Sir," the situation commander said. "Team three has her and she is secure in a room in Level 1."

"What the hell happened?" the frightened man said. "What the hell happened to Reynolds? What was that?"

"We're still not sure, Sir, but the building seems to be under some kind of attack. We haven't yet figured out what it is."

Several people were enjoying a late night visit in Lafayette Park across the street from the White House when the shooting started. They could not believe their eyes-or ears. As they sat quietly talking in the park two hundred yards from the White House fence, three terrific explosions, almost at the same time, went off behind them. The visitors could feel the concussion from the muzzle blasts and the sound was deafening. They turned to look and the three explosions went off again. By now, the park visitors were crouching down and covering their ears. When they faced the Hay Adams Hotel, they could see as well as feel the terrific concussion of these blasts. It appeared that some sort of cannons were being fired repeatedly at an unbelievably fast rate of fire out of windows in the upper floors of the Hay Adams at the White House! Because a terrific muzzle flash accompanied each firing, the park visitors could see that there were three guns at work. And the firing went on for a full two minutes, by which time each gun had fired forty rounds out of four ten-round magazines.

Within twenty seconds of the first rounds hitting the White House, Sirens began to wail, bright lights were turned on in every part of the White House grounds. Within three minutes, men in helmets ran back and forth behind the tall steel fence that surrounded the White House, and Humvees which must have been parked in some sort of underground facility roared into position at the various gates. The big Humvee trucks were armed with rocket launchers and machine guns and operators were poised behind their weapons. Within five minutes, large numbers of men began shuffling back and forth under the White House portico. They were building sandbag bunkers protecting more .50 caliber machine guns and rocket emplacements, which were just then being set up.

But the most spectacular sight of all was the White House itself, which appeared to be a large birthday cake festooned with candles. Small fires the size of flares appeared all over the roof and the walls of the building. Men appeared on the roof with fire extinguishers and began to put out the fires, but many of them burned brightly for twenty minutes. The White House had been penetrated with four hundred rounds of .50 caliber incendiary bullets and small and large fires burned brightly all over the huge building. The roof was full of holes and windows had been shattered all over the building.

In the situation room, three levels below the ground floor of the White House, the situation commander had received a communication from the ground commander that the attack seems to have been some sort of incendiary round fired from a great distance, possibly from a 20 mm cannon, or multiple 20 mm cannons.

Immediately, the situation commander went on a secure line to the emergency room of the Pentagon. "We have a Phase One alert at the White House," he said. "We are apparently under attack by multiple emplacements of 20 mm cannon. Dispatch Marine One. CICUS is on site and ready to go."

"Wilco," said the Pentagon operator. "ETA ten minutes."

Seven minutes later, the CICUS team whisked the president, who was now helmeted and kevlared head to toe, to a secure room near the landing zone. After another eight minutes, the team commander radioed the situation commander, "No helicopter yet."

"Stand by," the situation commander said.

The situation commander was back on the secure line to the Pentagon. "Where the hell is Marine One?"

"Sorry, situation room. Just got word. Mechanical problems. Suggest you put CICUS in a secure location until we can straighten this out."

"Are you insane? This is CICUS."

"I know who it is," the Pentagon said. "We'll call when we have something for you. But be advised that in response to your Phase One alert we have moved armored units into the area surrounding the White House and are in the process of sealing off the area. You are safe."

"Keep us advised," the situation commander said.

He then directed the presidential team to bring CICUS back to the bunker. When he arrived, the situation commander explained what the Pentagon had told him.

By three o'clock in the morning, the president had been waiting almost four hours for Marine One. "Get me the Chairman of the Joint Chiefs," Fuller said, furious.

A groggy General Buchanan answered the call that had been patched through to his home from the Pentagon. "Hello?"

"Buchanan, this is the president. What in the hell is going on? The White House is under some kind of attack. The vice president has been killed in front of me while he was sitting in my office, and although your emergency plans call for me to be taken by helicopter, I've been waiting for four hours to be evacuated. What in the hell are you doing?"

"Mr. President. We're on top of it. It's just a bizarre coincidence that Marine One failed while the backup is torn down in maintenance. We'll get to you. Just hang in there."

"Do you know what this attack is about?"

"Everybody is working on it," he said, stifling a yawn, "Just hang tight 'till we get to you." Without more, he hung up.

When the president called back to the Pentagon, the operator told him that the general was tied up and would speak with him soon.

Fuller slammed down the secure phone and looked around the room at the small army of secret service agents, who stared back at him in confusion. What the hell was happening?

32

The agency had supplied ten .50 caliber autoloaders and seven magazines holding ten rounds apiece. Sam had tested the guns and determined that a reasonably proficient operator could fire ten rounds in twenty seconds. If fifteen seconds were allowed to change magazines, each operator could fire forty rounds of incendiary .50 caliber ammunition in less than three minutes. Sam insisted, however, that each shooter be issued three additional magazines, or a total of seven magazines, in case he had to use the gun to extricate himself from trouble. The agency also supplied nine shooters. Sam was the tenth. If all ten shooters shot four magazines, the White House would be peppered with 400 .50 caliber incendiary bullets.

Three shooters were positioned across the street from the White House in the upper floors of the Hay Adams Hotel. One shooter was positioned in the Tidal Basin. One was on a roof on 14th St. N.W. One was on the roof of a George Washington University office building. And four, including Sam, were positioned in Arlington Cemetery. The cemetery shot appeared to be almost a mile. The other shots were much closer, with the Hay Adams shooters being almost on top of the target.

Sam and his three CIA colleagues arrived in the Arlington Cemetery about nine thirty the night before martial law was to go into effect. They had left their specially prepared SUV and driver alongside the road in an emergency pull-off and they had hiked into position in the cemetery. Each of the shooters picked his own position to shoot from. Each had a clear view of the White House. Each shooter was within twenty-five yards of the others, some higher, some lower in on the hill of the cemetery. All fired from the prone position, two using the bipod built into the forend of the rifle, two using a free-standing tripod that achieved a little more height. All were equipped with electronic earmuffs which also had internal closed-circuit communicators. At about eleven o'clock Sam said into the communicator, "Ears on. Fire when ready on my mark." Within thirty seconds, the muzzle blast from Sam's first round started the volley. Within two seconds, the other three shooters began firing. Within three minutes, each of the four shooters had shot forty rounds of .50 caliber incendiary ammunition into the White House and fires were blazing all over the roof, in interior walls where windows had been penetrated, and in exterior walls and roofs.

The Secret Service, in preparation for the implementation of martial law, had begun a series of roving patrols within a five-mile radius of the White House. One of these Secret Service units was crossing the Arlington Memorial Bridge when the alarm was announced on its radio that the White House had been attacked. Simultaneously, the two agents saw brilliant flashes erupting from what looked like one of the hills of the Arlington Cemetery. The agents immediately called in their observation and headed for the cemetery.

By the time the Secret Service agents had crashed their black Suburban through the fence surrounding the road barrier at the Arlington Memorial Cemetery entrance, Sam and the other operatives had completed their mission and were packing up. Empty brass, some of it still scalding hot, went into canvas bags attached to battle harnesses. Bipods and tripods were collapsed, emergency magazines were inserted into the magazine wells of the big rifles, and the rifles were slung over shoulders as the group of four shooters began the hike back to the waiting car.

The sound of the 454 cubic inch Suburban was audible long before they saw the car racing toward them. The men were well trained. They scattered and dropped to the ground, unslinging the rifles as they did, and rolling into a firing position. Two of the men were firing at the advancing Suburban before Sam got his first shot off. Sam's shot, which shattered the engine block, was probably unnecessary. Several incendiary rounds had hit the front of the engine compartment and the windscreen and penetrated both. The engine locked up almost instantaneously and the driver was killed when a .50 caliber round penetrated the windshield and tore off one side of his head. The car crashed and the other agent remained motionless inside, the lower half of his body missing from the shrapnel that burst through the firewall when the engine block disintegrated.

The operators slung their thirty-pound rifles again and headed off toward the waiting SUV. As they descended the hill near where it was parked, they could see on the other side of a hedgerow that their SUV was still there, but it was flanked by three metropolitan police cars with red and blue lights flashing.

A voice on a loudspeaker was ordering the driver to step out of the car. Apparently he wasn't moving, because the frustrated voice kept demanding that he get out of the car.

The operatives looked at Sam. He made hand signals for a flanking movement, sending two men to the left, and he with one man went to the right.

"Ready on the left," came the sound into the headset.

"Wait one," Sam muttered, struggling to find a place for a clear shot.

Sam checked his partner on the right and then said, "O.K. now. Ready on the right. Fire on my mark."

Twenty seconds later, Sam's fifty caliber rifle boomed and within milliseconds, the three other rifles began as well. The police cars were rendered inoperative with the first shots, and three of the six policemen who manned them lay dead. Thirty-five rounds of .50 caliber incendiaries hit the police cars and the policemen. Fifteen seconds after the firing had started, everything was eerily quiet and dark. The flashing lights were gone, shattered, the police cars were smoldering dark wreckages, and the demanding voice on the loudspeaker was quiet.

33

After the president had waited four hours for his helicopter and been rebuffed by General Buchanan when he demanded to be extracted from the White House, he began to come unraveled. He seemed to wilt. His only supporter, the vice president, was dead. His other supporters on the cabinet could not get through the blockade. Even his wife was being held in a separate area, as was called for by the evacuation plan. He was the president, but he didn't seem to be in control.

Finally, the president dozed off in a chair, and when he awakened thirty minutes later, seemed to be uncertain of himself.

"Do you think we could drive out of here?" he said uncertainly to the agent in charge.

"If that's what you want to do, Sir, we'll do it."

"I'd like to go to Camp David," the president mumbled.

"The cars will be ready in ten minutes, Mr. President."

Twenty minutes later, agents helped the president, who now appeared to be almost a feeble old man, into the back of his armored limousine. Once again, he was plastered with Kevlar and vests with steel plates. It was incongruous to see him hobbling along, bundled up in these bulky garments with wisps of his white hair under the helmet he was wearing, which was tightly strapped to his chin.

The presidential convoy proceeded out of the front gate led by two armored Suburbans. The lead car was fitted with a .30 caliber mini-gun that was mounted on a hydraulic platform that emerged through the roof when activated. The gun fired at 1,500 rounds per minute. The operator stood behind the gun and was protected by the roof panels that stood up on end to his right and his left, creating the hole in the roof through which the gun emerged.

Behind the lead Suburban came the command car, fitted with a remotely controlled .50 caliber machine gun that emerged through the roof at the back of the car. The gunner, who was also the convoy commander, sat in the passenger seat, where he faced a targeting screen. On his left was the command communications equipment for the convoy.

Following the command car, came Cadillac One, the presidential limousine, which was a Cadillac body fitted to a GMC truck body. It's armour included glass that was five inches thick. It was powered by a specially tuned Cadillac 454 cubic inch engine and an all-wheel drive transmission.

Following Cadillac One came three more armored Suburbans, including one with extensive medical equipment and a doctor.

The presidential convoy pulled up to the barricade at 17th Street and Pennsylvania Avenue. Passage was blocked by an M-1 Abrams tank which was flanked by two Bradley M3A3 Fighting Vehicles. The Bradleys were fitted with heavy machine guns and 20 mm chain guns and they seemed to be performing the duty of protecting their heavier partner, the M1 tank, much as destroyers protect battle ships.

The Bradleys were heavily armoured tracked vehicles capable of extreme maneuverability, weighing 30 tons. They were powered by 600 horsepower diesel engines and were served by a crews of three, the commander, a driver and a gunner. These Bradleys were also carrying six battle-ready soldiers.

The M-1 tank weighs seventy tons and is powered by a 1500 horsepower gas turbine engine. This particular tank was fitted with four main weapons, the 105mm rifled tank gun and three machine guns including a .30 caliber M 240, mounted alongside the main gun and fired from inside the tank using the main gun's sights. The M 240 is used for engaging soft targets when the operator does not want to use the main gun.

"This is Checkpoint 17 to command," the tank commander said into his radio.

"Command."

"The presidential motorcade is coming this way."

"Orders are confirmed. No ingress or egress. No exceptions. Code alpha." Code alpha made the order a matter of national security, which was to be carried out at any cost.

"Does this apply to the presidential vehicle as well."

"It applies to every vehicle. That intersection is closed and the code is alpha. Clean out your ears, soldier."

The driver of the first Suburban leaned out his window and yelled, "Hey guys, open up. It's the president."

Nothing.

The Suburban blew its siren. Nothing.

Then the tank's turret began to move. The 105mm rifled tank gun and its coaxial mounted .30 caliber M240 machine gun slowly rotated until it was pointed directly at the lead Suburban. As the tank's main gun began to rotate, the Bradleys moved forward on each side of the tank and blocked the intersection completely.

"Are you insane?" the secret service agent bellowed into the loudspeaker fitted into the truck he was driving.

With the turret guns pointed directly at the lead Suburban, the tank commander's hatch opened and the commander, a marine captain, emerged from the hatch. He made a motion for the agent to roll down his window. The ashen-faced agent complied.

"Can't come through here, sir," the captain said.

"This is the president's convoy," the agent said.

"I'm aware of what it is, sir."

"Then get the hell out of the way and get that gun out of my face."

"Sorry, sir. Orders are that no one goes in or out."

"That can't apply to the president, you idiot."

"It applies to everyone, sir."

"Let me speak to your commanding officer."

"I am the commanding officer, sir."

"If you value your commission, you'll move these vehicles out of the way."

"Sorry, sir. I told you. No one goes in or out.

The agent rolled up his window and radioed the convoy commander.

"Sir, they won't let us through."

"Ask to speak to the commanding officer," the convoy commander said.

"I did," the agent said. "He's the guy who told me we can't go through."

"Drive around he sonofabitch," the convoy commander yelled.

"Sir?"

"You heard me. Drive up on the sidewalk through those bushes, and engage that goddam tank with your machine gun. I'm going to hit them with the .50. The convoy will be right behind you."

"Sir. These are tanks."

"Do what you're fucking told, agent."

"Yes sir."

The driver of the lead Suburban hit the switch that raised the .30 caliber mini-gun through the roof. The operator rode up through the roof with the gun and as the roof panels locked open and the gun's platform clunked into position the operator used foot pedals to rotate the gun toward the closest Bradley. The driver accelerated the Suburban toward the outside of the Bradley on the tank's right, heading for a row of bushes alongside a sidewalk, hoping to open a path over the sidewalk and through the bushes for the rest of the convoy. As the Suburban hit the curb, the mini-gunner opened up on the Bradley, which now was moving to intersect them. Black exhaust smoke billowed from the Bradley's rear-mounted stack as the Bradley's driver accelerated the big diesel on a collision course with the Suburban.

The sound of the Suburban's .30 mini-gun was roughly like a deafening ripping of fabric. At 1,500 rounds per minute, the gun fired so fast that individual detonations of the rounds could not be identified. It was one long, drawn-out ripping or buzzing sound. Brass from the mini-gun poured out the ejection port so rapidly that it was piling up on the windshield and the driver had to actuate the windshield wipers to be able to see. The mini-gun was firing in bursts, one ripping sound, then another, then another, then another, with brass flying all over and finally pinging off the pavement and coming to rest in great piles.

The thirty caliber rounds were hitting the Bradley and deflecting. It was hard to figure out whether more sound was coming from the rip of the mini-gun or from the clanging of hundreds of bullets against the Bradley. The sound of .30 caliber armour piercing bullets hitting the Bradley at 1,500 rounds per minute was like the sound of a crowd of people banging on metal trashcans with hammers. Ricochets were later found in buildings three blocks away. None of the rounds penetrated the Bradley, but the sound inside the M3A3 was horrendous and deafening. It seemed likely the rounds would pierce the armour at any moment, that they would actually drill through the steel plate by sheer repetition of hit after hit in the same place.

The driver of the Bradley pivoted the 30-ton monster, locking one tread and driving with the other, to plow into the lead Suburban. With the throttle wide open, he hit the Suburban at a forty-five degree angle just as the car's rear wheels bumped over the curb, trying to flank the war machine. When the Bradley hit the Suburban, it's tread on the left dug into the left front fender of the car, bringing the car to an abrupt jarring halt, throwing the mini-gun operator out of the turret onto the pavement, and mashing both agents in the front of the car into their seat belts and the windscreen. The Bradley then opened up with its own machine guns and pulverized the windscreen of the Suburban killing both agents at once.

As this was happening, the command Suburban had actuated the remotely controlled .50 caliber machine gun, which had appeared through the roof of the second Suburban. Much like the mini-gun in the first car, the .50 appeared on top of the car and was flanked by the opened roof panels. Like the mini-gun also, it rotated on a turret to engage its target. It was, however, remotely controlled, and no operator was visible. The gunner was in the passenger seat.

When the Bradley dug its tread into the first Suburban, the convoy commander in the second Suburban opened up with the .50, firing directly at the Bradley that had stopped the first Suburban. He got off three rounds before everything went black. The other Bradley on the right flank of the tank had fired two rounds from its 20 mm chain gun into the second Suburban. The Suburban erupted in a ball of flame and there was a loud whump from the ignition of gasoline. The 20mm rounds had penetrated the Suburban through and through and had destroyed everything, instantly, human and non-human.

Simultaneously, the second Bradley lurched forward when the column started to move, smashing broadside into the driver's door of Cadillac One and nearly tipping it over. Cadillac One was impaled on the front of the Bradley at a thirty-degree angle, resting on the two wheels of the passenger side.

The M1 commander, acting as combat supervisor, monitored the action, and when the command Suburban exploded, out of the corner of his eye, he caught the movement of the Gatling gun operator, who had been thrown clear of the crash with the Bradley, crawling away. The M1 commander quickly swiveled the turret and cut the man in half with his M240 machine gun. An alpha order meant that lockdown was absolute and that anyone who threatened to breach the checkpoint was to be killed.

When the Bradley hit the president's car, the president was first slammed against the door to his left, and then slid to the right down the seat to the bottom end of the upended car. His two agents were on top of him. Had he not been wearing a helmet, he would have been injured. As it was, he and two secret service agents riding with him were in a pile at the lower end of the car that was being held in place at a severe angle by the second Bradley Fighting Vehicle.

Underneath the weight of his two agents, Fuller thought he would die either of compression or suffocation. He couldn't move. He couldn't breathe. Two large men weighing two hundred pounds apiece were on top of him. Suddenly, there was a loud screeching noise as the Bradley backed up and disengaged itself from the underside of Cadillac One, allowing it to bump to the ground with all four wheels in place. The agents scrambled off the president and tried to pull him back into a seated position, but all the while he was flailing and gasping for breath and crying, "What's happening? You're supposed to protect me? What's going on?"

"You're all right now, Mr. President," one agent said. "Just calm down."

"Goddam it. Calm down. Fucking Calm down? Get me the hell out of here," the president bellowed.

The driver cranked the wheel of Cadillac one and jammed the throttle to the floor. The 700 horsepower modified engine responded with a guttural scream and all wheels churning. A dented, scraped, singed and pock-marked Cadillac One skidded around the smoking wreckage of the two Suburbans. The cars behind Cadillac One hastily followed.

For the next twenty minutes, what was left of the convoy circled the White House, looking for a way out. Military vehicles blocked every road, intersection, alley, and sidewalk. As the convoy passed the checkpoints, the turrets of the tanks and fighting vehicles followed them until they were past. Finally, the convoy returned to the White House. A sobbing and distraught president had to be helped inside.

Back in the situation room, the president shed his armor and sank into a chair. His face was red and his hands were trembling as he asked for the telephone and dialed Buchanan's direct number. Once again, maddeningly, he got a Pentagon emergency officer.

"I'm calling for General Buchanan," a frightened, exasperated, annoyed, exhausted and infuriated president said.

"Yes sir, please hold."

What was happening? The president is put on hold? The military won't allow the president to pass through a roadblock? They kill my bodyguards? They shoot guns at me? The White House is sealed off from the outside world? Bombs are shot into the White House? The vice president is dead. . . .

Buchanan's voice came on the phone. "Mr. President," he said.

"What the hell is going on?" the president screamed, all of his fear, exhaustion, and dread coming out all at once.

"What do you mean, Sir? There's been an attack on the White House and we are taking protective measures."

"What protective measures?" the president was pretending to an authority he now wasn't sure he still had. "You won't send my helicopter. You kill my bodyguards. You shoot guns at me. You won't let me drive to Camp David. And I'm supposed to be the goddam Commander in Chief."

"Yes, Sir."

"Is that it? Yes, Sir?"

"No, Sir. A Congressional delegation is on its way in to see you. They have just passed the checkpoint at Pennsylvania Avenue. They should be there in a few minutes."

"What the hell is that? How can they get in and I can't get out?" The phone went dead.

The color was now gone from the president's face. He slumped a little in his chair and closed his eyes. He couldn't think straight. He was scared. He was exhausted. They were trying to kill him. Buchanan must be in on it. They all wanted him dead. They all . . .

A secret service agent touched his arm and put a cup of tea on the desk in front of him.

"Sir, I thought you might need a cup of tea," the agent said.

"Thanks," the president said distractedly. "A Congressional delegation is coming in. Show them into the conference room down here, will you?"

"Yes sir."

Twenty minutes later, Fuller entered the underground conference room. The table was large enough to seat forty people. The Congressional delegation consisted of ten senators and Congressmen. Fuller noticed that the Attorney General was also there. As Fuller entered the room, everyone stood. He made a gesture for them to sit, and wearily, he took his seat at the head of the table.

"Gentlemen," he said. "It seems that you can get in but I can't get out."

There was silence.

"What can I do for you," he finally said.

Mason, the Speaker of the House, said, "Mr. President, we are here to serve you with articles of impeachment. I am sorry to have to tell you that."

There was silence again. Air rushed through the underground air supply system. Tension and fear ran through the room.

Fuller couldn't make his brain work right. Impeachment. Why? Are they in it too? Are they going to kill me right here? How did things come to this? I spent my whole life . . .

Fuller found himself saying, "Why now?"

"A crisis is imminent," Mason said. "And an immediate solution is needed to avoid what we believe will be a civil war."

Fuller couldn't see quite right. Mason was blurred. Fuller almost felt like giggling. Civil war? They were all crazy. Fuller felt himself dissolving, falling apart, crumbling. He forced himself to look around the room at the others. He had to appear normal. They couldn't know he couldn't see clearly. He felt dizzy. He gripped the arms of his chair. There was no way he could stand up.

"And what makes you think that, Mr. Mason?" he managed to say.

"The executive order you signed banning the possession of firearms, as you know, has sparked violence and disregard for law and order in every part of the country."

"That's it? Criminals shoot the police and you impeach the president?"

"It's not just the gun ban, Mr. President. You also have ordered martial law and the deployment of military forces into all of the nation's major cities. We believe that the two things together-the gun ban and martial law-will throw the country into civil war. . . . And we believe that you acted beyond your authority in ordering the gun ban in the first place. It goes without saying that the martial law declaration was illegal because it was based on the illegal gun ban."

At some point during Mason's explanation, Fuller lost the ability to understand what was being said. Now the words as well as what he was seeing were blurred. He said nothing when Mason stopped talking. He prayed he would not get so dizzy that he fell out of the chair.

"Mr. President," Mason continued, "

"You can't do this, you know," Fuller mumbled.

The room was silent again.

"Are you all crazy? The White House has been bombed. The vice president is dead. There are tanks and troops all over the streets. And you want to impeach the president? What's wrong with you? What about national security? What about protecting the president and the constitution? Are you insane?"

"Mr. President," the Attorney General said, "the general feeling is that these things have happened because of your actions."

"You can't be right Mr. Carnegie. I carry out the duties of my office and you blame me for the illegal acts of those who don't like it."

"The view of the delegation, Mr. President, is that you broke the law. You exceeded your authority. You created a situation in which the continued viability of the country was thrown into question," the Attorney General said.

"And what do you think?" Fuller said.

"I agree with them, Mr. President. I advised you not to impose the gun ban from the first," the Attorney General said.

"So, you intend to remove me from office," Fuller said, seeming to regain some of his faculties.

"Yes, Sir," Mason said.

"And it is you, Mr. Mason, who would benefit most from this because you, as Speaker of the House, would become president yourself," Fuller said.

"I take no pleasure in that, Mr. President," Mason said. "It is with sadness that I come here today"

"I'm sure," the president said. After thinking for a minute, he said, "The essence of what you are charging me with is what?"

The Attorney General said, "Malfeasance in office. It is the belief of the

Congress that you have risked the catastrophe of a civil war in an attempt to further your personal agenda of banning guns."

"My personal agenda. . . " Fuller said. "Am I the only one in this room who has heard of gun violence?"

Mason said, "You appear to be the only one in this room who has not heard of the Second Amendment and of the inherent right of self-defense."

Fuller laughed. "I'm the one who has to be concerned about self-defense. I can see that you're all in this together. You, the Congress, my own Attorney General, the military. . . You're all conspirators. You, not I, are acting illegally. You are trying to overthrow the government. For all I know, you killed the vice president."

As he spoke, the president seemed to gain self-confidence. He sat up straighter. He could see more clearly. He got a surge of energy. He knew what they were doing. They were not going to get away with it.

"Mr. President," Mason said, "this is not a coup. We are removing you from office by legal and constitutional means."

"You're a little ahead of yourself, aren't you, Mr. Mason. Don't you have to have the trial before you remove me from office?"

"With respect, Sir," Mason continued. "We know the result. We have canvassed the House and the Senate and the vote is overwhelmingly for impeachment."

"Things can change," Fuller said. "A trial may cause people to think otherwise."

"We do not intend to have a trial in the ordinary sense of that term, Mr. President. There are only two questions before the Congress in this impeachment. The first is whether you imposed the gun ban. The second is whether you ordered martial law. If the answer to both questions is in the affirmative, you will be impeached as a matter of law. We are treating your actions as questions of strict liability. If you did these things, you are impeachable as a matter of law."

"Do you agree with this, Carnegie?" Fuller said.

"Yes, Sir. I do. Both of these actions have threatened to throw the country into chaos, the very opposite of what a president is supposed to do. If you acted without realizing the consequences, then you are incompetent. If you acted knowing the consequences, then you must be removed from office because of malfeasance."

Mason said, "Mr. President, because the outcome of this impeachment trial is certain and because time is of the essence, we have prepared a document for you in which you agree to resign from office, effective immediately, in exchange for the withdrawal of impeachment charges against you."

The president appeared to shrink in his chair. The adrenaline surge had worn off. Fear and self-doubt returned. His vision blurred again. He couldn't focus clearly.

Finally, Fuller said, "I don't care what you call it, this is a coup. You are all traitors."

"Mr. President," Carnegie said, "from the earliest days of this republic, dating back to the Declaration of Independence, it has been the law and the tradition of this country that if the government were to become oppressive, not in small things, but in large things, it is the right and the duty of the people to remove that government by whatever means are available to them."

"You're criminals and traitors," the president erupted. "John," he yelled to the agent in charge, "arrest everyone in this room."

"Mr. President," the Attorney General said, "consider what you are doing."

Fuller stared blindly into space. Again he was overcome with exhaustion and fear. He had the feeling a line had been crossed. Things had gone too far. A heaviness overcame him. He was confused. He didn't know what to do next. Secret service agents filled the room.

"Mr. President," the agent in charge said, "What do you want me to do?"

"Just wait," Fuller said, holding his head in his hands.

"Mr. President," the Attorney General said. "I suggest we take a break from these negotiations and that you call General Buchanan."

"What will he tell me?" Fuller mumbled, wearily.

"He didn't say. But he asked me to have you call him if we reached an impasse."

"John," Fuller said, "take these people to the other conference room. No one is to leave."

"Yes, Sir."

The delegation of Congressmen filed out accompanied by the Attorney General and fifteen secret service agents. The White House kitchen fed them sandwiches and cold drinks. When they were gone, Fuller dialed Buchanan's number. This time Buchanan answered himself.

"Hello, Mr. President."

"They told me to call you." The president's voice was empty, distracted.

"Yes. I gather you've reached an impasse."

"If you call betrayal of one's country an impasse, then yes we have."

"There is a man you need to meet with."

"Who?"

"His name is Sam Budda. He will be passed through the Pennsylvania

Avenue checkpoint within the hour."
"What is the purpose of this meeting?
The phone went dead.

34

Sam Budda, accompanied by a Colonel in the Military Police, walked through the checkpoint at 17th and Pennsylvania Avenue, and then walked down the street toward the White House. The street was empty. Deserted. Quiet. Ominous. Only the sounds of military radios crackled in the night. As he approached the White House, he saw activity in the grounds. He couldn't tell exactly what was going on, but there was both mechanized maneuvering and the movement of men on foot.

Sam stood at the main gate of the White House an hour after the president had talked with General Buchanan. Flack jacketed Secret Service guards opened the big iron gate just enough to let him in. The colonel who had accompanied Sam wished him luck and turned back in the direction they had come. Sam was allowed to pass through the White House gate and then was immediately pushed to the ground and frisked while three guards pointed .30 caliber rifles at his head. Two guards patted Sam down and a third scanned him with a portable scanner, and then they pronounced him clean.

"Orders," one of the guards said, offering Sam a hand to get up.

"Thanks," Sam said. He brushed off his corduroy pants and his bush jacket, which was covered with debris from the driveway. Four guards led him to the main entrance of the White House.

At the door, Sam was turned over to the plainclothes agents, who, once again, put him on the floor and frisked him, then scanned him with two separate scanners. They took his belt and his keys. They then blindfolded him and led him to an elevator, where he could feel that they were descending. When the door opened, they removed the blindfold and Sam saw that he was in a wide hallway surrounded by at least twelve guards, some of whom were carrying submachine guns.

They led him down the hall and through two rooms before coming to the room in which the president was. The president was seated in a large leather lounge chair in front of a fireplace with a blazing fire. It was almost as if he had been transported to a cabin in the mountains. The president, haggard and worn out, turned to face Sam and got up from his chair.

"Who are you?" Fuller said.

"Sam Budda."

"Who is that?"

"Just someone who has been asked to speak with you."

"About what?"

"About your options."

"You think I don't know my options?"

"Correct."

There was something about Sam's demeanor that gave Fuller pause. He was not arrogant. He was not threatening. He was not . . . anything. Just a man. There was also something engaging about this man. Maybe it was the unusual situation. Maybe Fuller was just too exhausted to know what he was doing. He motioned for Sam to sit in the other chair facing the fire and he sat himself.

"Why you, Mr. Budda? Who are you?"

"A government contractor."

"You work for a federal agency?"

"Yes."

"Doing what?"

"I'm sorry, Sir. That's classified."

"Fuller gave a mirthless snort and said, "Have you forgotten, Mr. Budda. I'm the president."

"Yes, Sir. You're entitled to know anything you want, just not from me. I am pledged to secrecy."

"All right, Mr. Budda. You're a man of principle. Now what is it you want to tell me?"

"First of all, Sir, we need to have his conversation in private."

"You want my protective detail to leave?"

"Yes, sir."

"How do I know you won't harm me?"

"Ask one of your agents to leave you his gun. You know I am unarmed."

Fuller thought for a moment, and then said, "John, leave us alone."

"Mr. President? I can't do that."

"Do it John," the president said, a tired impatience in his voice.

Shaking his head, the lead agent and two others left the room, leaving Sam and Fuller alone.

"I believe you were going to explain my options," Fuller said, somewhat testily.

"Before we get to that, we need to talk about some mistakes you made."

"Mistakes?"

"Yes.

"If I had to guess, I would guess you grew up in a wealthy family and went to a private boarding school."

"Yes, I did. So what"

"And for the last twenty years of your political career, you have been protected either by the capital police or the secret service.

"Yes. So what?"

"And wherever you lived before you moved into the White House, crime was not much of a concern."

"Where are you going with this?"

"And I'll bet your kids were not bussed to school."

"They were not. So what."

"Your first mistake is that you do not believe anyone is seriously concerned about self-defense because you yourself have never had to be concerned about self defense."

"That's right. I don't and I haven't. That's what the police are for."

"Well, Sir, the police have their functions, but preventing crime isn't one of them. And, begging your pardon, Sir, the only reason you think the police can protect people is they protect you. Basically, you are selfish. Security isn't a concern for you, so it shouldn't be a concern for anyone else."

Fuller chuckled, "If the police don't protect people, Mr. Budda, what do they do?"

"They investigate the crimes they couldn't prevent."

"Why do you say they can't prevent crimes?"

"I don't say that Mr. President. They do. Use your head. A crime occurs within seconds, or at the most, minutes, in secret, in the dark, where no one but the victim knows. How do the police prevent that?"

"That's never been my experience, Mr. Budda."

"Of course not. That's my point. How could it be your experience when you are surrounded by police. You don't need to dial 911. The police are already there. But the rest of the world doesn't have that luxury."

"What's my second mistake, Mr. Budda?"

"Your second mistake stems from the first. You believe that no one fears the government. And you think that if they do fear the government, they are nut cases."

"I guess that's pretty much right, but how's it related to the first so-called mistake."

"The two mistakes come from the same place. They come from the fact that you can't see beyond your own privileged position. You think that because you don't fear crime and you don't fear the government, there is no reason for anyone else to be afraid. It's unimaginable to you that the BATF would barge into your bedroom and, at the point of guns, pull you and your wife out of bed and throw you on the floor. But if you thought that might happen, you'd be just as afraid of the government as other people are."

"What's my third mistake?"

"You are a typical politician in that you don't believe in anything. This doesn't make you unique, of course, but when you're the president, you have to keep your cynicism in check. It is common knowledge you are on this gun crusade just for votes, just because it's popular with a certain segment of to population, and not because you think it's right. And you're willing to allow agencies like BATF to become tyrannical in the service of your vote getting."

"I don't run the BATF. It's not my job to supervise how they do theirs. If they have misbehaved, then that's what the courts are for. It not a reason for rebellion."

"That's a really good theoretical answer, Mr. President, but ordinary people know that in order to use the courts, you have to have money. And not only that, but when the government arrests people and causes them to lose their jobs, these people need to figure out some way to support themselves for four or five years while the courts get around to figuring things out."

"That's the system," Fuller said.

"That's your system. That's the system for people who have the money and privilege you have always had. It's not the system for ordinary people. When you beat them up and invade their homes and take their property and terrorize their families and destroy a person's ability to make a living, all because he has a gun you don't like, you better not count on any ordinary person to be satisfied with waiting for the courts to sort it out."

"So tell me again," Fuller said, "What's wrong with getting votes?"

"Your job as president is not to get votes; it is to provide leadership within the framework of the constitution. That constitution, as you know, contains a Second Amendment. And the Supreme Court, as you know, has interpreted the Second Amendment to protect gun ownership, the very thing you want to stamp out. You have been short-sighted and irresponsible in placing votes ahead of doing what you knew was right."

"Are these all my mistakes?"

"They're the ones I know about that led to the current situation."

"Let's suppose, for the sake of argument, that you are right, that people believe strongly in self-defense, that they fear the government, and that they don't like the way I implement some of my ideas. So what? Every president has people that disagree with him."

"With respect, Mr. President, that is why you are such a dangerous man. You think your gun policies and your declaration of martial law and your encouragement of thug behavior in federal law enforcement agencies are just ordinary things that people can disagree about. You don't understand the fear of an overreaching government. You don't understand the fear of standing by helplessly while you are victimized by criminals or by agents of your own government. And you don't understand these things because you don't imagine that you yourself would ever be affected by them. But the people who wrote the Declaration of Independence understood those feelings, and they acted on them. In other words, Mr. President, although you don't see it yourself, the government you have created is so oppressive that it is tyrannical."

"Ah, this is your considered judgment, Mr. Budda?"

"No, Sir. It is the judgment of the key members of your government. I am just the messenger."

"The messenger of what?"

"Of your options."

"O.K. Let's stop wasting time. What are my options?"

"Resign or be forced to resign."

"So far you haven't told me anything that the people before you didn't tell me."

"They probably didn't emphasize that you need to make that decision right now."

"What do you mean?"

"As time goes on there will be a continuation of the ongoing battles between citizens who have broken no laws and the police."

"That doesn't seem to me to be a matter of much concern."

"That is because you don't appreciate what will happen when those old men who have become folk heroes ramp up their campaign against the government. At some point, you will be involved in a full blown civil war."

"That's speculation, Mr. Budda."

"Yes, Sir, it is. But you already have several thousand incidents of people resisting police who want to take their guns. As the number of these incidents increases, armed resistance will become the normal response, and when that happens, we will have civil war."

"So your idea is that if I resign, these policies can be reversed. What if I reversed them myself?"

"That wouldn't work. No one that has been involved in the resistance would believe you."

"What if I refuse to resign? I don't really believe that the Congress can pull off an impeachment trial where I don't even get a chance to present a defense."

"You may be right."

"Why then, shouldn't I just wait for the impeachment proceedings?"

"Because you wouldn't make it to the proceedings."

For the first time in the conversation, fear swept over the president. He hadn't liked what Budda had said and had even been angered by it, but Budda's pleasant, easy manner had lulled him into thinking of Budda as a friend, almost a confidant. Now Fuller looked at Sam in an effort to see signs that violence was imminent or signs of hatred, or some indication of anger or emotion of any kind. He saw nothing.

"You mean you would kill me?" Fuller said, hesitantly.

"I couldn't protect you. No one could. You saw what happened to your vice president. That could have been you."

"Are you a trained killer?"

"I have killed people."

"Are you here to kill me?"

"I'm here to save your life. You need to sign the resignation.

As Fuller looked at Sam, a sense of inevitability swept over him. He wasn't going to talk his way out of this. He wasn't going to be able to stonewall. He couldn't lie. And they wouldn't let him put it off. Or maybe they would.

"Let me think about it," Fuller ventured, hesitantly.

"I need your answer now," Sam said.

"What if I lied to you?"

"You can't lie to a bullet," Sam said.

Budda was talking in riddles, but the message was clear: Fuller would resign or he would die. Budda was five feet away and he would kill him, but Fuller wanted to live. There was no point in continuing this charade. He couldn't win. Budda was right about his privileged life. Maybe people did fear crime and the government and maybe he was wrong to take away their only means of defense. In any event, he wasn't going to be able to talk himself out of this.

"Give me the paper."

Sam handed Fuller a copy of the document prepared by the Congressional delegation and watched as Thurmond Fuller signed it, resigning as President of the United States. It seemed a momentous occasion, but there were no brass bands, no television networks, and no ceremony. There were no crowds, no farewell speeches, and no sobbing staffers. Even the reporting of this historic event would have to come later, for there were not even any newspaper reporters.

At Sam's request, Fuller called the secret service agents back in the room, and several of them witnessed the signature. Afterward, realizing that Fuller was no longer the president, they stood around awkwardly. When the last agent had signed, Fuller excused himself, leaving Sam with the signed document in which Thurmond Fuller relinquished his claim to the most powerful public office in the world.

35

At noon the next day, the world watched as Rutherford Mason was sworn in by the Chief Justice of the United States as President of the United States. The ceremony was conducted on the grounds of the Capital. When the last words of the oath were broadcast, a cheer went up from the crowd and Mason, beaming, waved from his position on an elevated platform.

The news of Fuller's resignation in the midst of an attack on the White House stunned everyone. What had really happened? Why did he resign? Was he forced to resign? Did they hold a gun to his head? How could they? He was surrounded by the Secret Service. Was there some dark secret from his past? Was he ill? Or was he just tired? But why now? Why all of a sudden?

News anchors and pundits debated these questions endlessly, preempting normal programming. Competing for airtime was coverage of the diminishing military presence in Washington, the massive M-1 tanks and armored personnel carriers climbing aboard flatbed trucks to be transported back to holding areas. The troops left Washington and every other city in large troop transport trucks, and the National Guard was ordered to stand down. The national news media filmed these events and discussed them in amazement. The country seemed to be returning to normal. SWAT trucks were nowhere to be seen.

President Mason held a press conference in the late afternoon at which he made a short statement and then answered questions for an hour. In his statement he announced that the executive order banning firearms had been rescinded, as had the declaration of martial law. Federal troops had been ordered back to their bases and firearms seized during the recent police actions were ordered returned to their owners. Property owners who had suffered damage because of police actions on their property were directed to an office in Homeland Security to present claims for the damage. Families of persons who were killed or persons who were injured during the recent police actions to seize firearms were directed to another office to make their claims.

Then the blockbuster announcements. Jesse Washington and Jamie Berenger were pardoned from any and all prosecutions which had been brought or would be brought on account of the recent police actions. Mulhaney was also pardoned. And finally, the BATF was abolished forthwith and its duties and responsibilities would be shared by Homeland Security and the FBI.

Then the questions:

"Mr. President," John Blather of CBS said, "isn't all of this just giving in to the gun lobby?"

"Mr. Blather, none of the actions I have taken have anything to do with the gun lobby. It was the right thing to do. President Fuller had acted precipitously and illegally in imposing a gun ban and martial law."

"Are you a gun rights supporter?" Mimi Johnson of CNN asked.

"Ms. Johnson, I support the Constitution. As you know, the Constitution has a Second Amendment, and the Supreme Court has determined that it provides for the private ownership of firearms and for the right of self-defense. My job is to enforce that decision. I am not going to try to end-run the Supreme Court by writing an Executive Order banning guns and then ask them to reconsider what they have already decided.

"Besides that, Ms. Johnson, remember that we have a two hundred year history of gun ownership in this country, and remember that when this country was formed, there was much concern among those who wrote the Declaration of Independence and the Constitution that the new government should not turn into a tyrant like the one they were just then escaping, and that if the new government did become tyrannical, the people should have some means of resisting it. This meant guns.

"So when you ask whether I am a gun rights supporter, Ms. Johnson, my answer is that I support the Constitution and the rule of law. It is for other branches of government, not the Executive Branch, to determine the role of guns in our society."

"Why did you pardon Jesse Washington and Jamie Berenger, who are self-confessed killers?" Sheffield Rock of the Washington Post asked.

"Mr. Rock," the president said, "these men are, in my opinion, national heroes. They knew what the BATF was doing was wrong, and they knew what former President Fuller was doing was wrong. In both cases, the government was acting as a tyrant, and they resisted.

"Of course, my heart goes out to the families of those who were killed because of the actions of these men, but if these courageous men had not resisted the tyranny that former President Fuller had implemented, we might at this moment be living in a defacto police state, or we might be engaged in a civil war. These men provided the leadership that prevented that from happening."

"Mr. President," Mary Ballinski, of the New York Times, said, "what about Mulhaney. He was convicted by a jury."

"Mulhaney was just an unfortunate victim of BATF excesses. How he got convicted, I'll never understand, but in any case, he is now free."

"How do you feel, taking the most powerful office in the world without having been elected while the man who was elected seems to have been forced out?" Barbara Peters, of the Pittsburgh Post Gazette, asked.

"Ms. Peters, I am saddened by the way in which I was elevated to this office. I take no pleasure in it and I am sobered by it. On the other hand, I thank God that former President Fuller was not allowed to go on unchecked, for if he had, I firmly believe that the nation would have been plunged into civil war."

"Mr. President," James Loughin of NVC news said, "isn't your gun policy a slap in the face of every community in the United States who has sought to ban guns?"

"Mr. Loughin, is it? These communities, as you call them, are a slap in the face of the American people. These communities have attempted to avoid the Second Amendment on the theory that removing guns from everyone will put an end to gun violence. Frankly, Mr. Loughin, that is stupid. If their gun bans went into effect, criminals would still have guns and the gun violence that the cities are trying to avoid would still be with them. What these communities need to do is enforce the laws that prohibit gun violence, and then they won't have it."

"Ladies and gentlemen, that's all for now, it has been a long day."

The new president left in the midst of a large detail of Secret Service agents, who surrounded him. He left to cheers and clapping uncharacteristic of the press corps.

* * *

The next afternoon, Jesse Washington and Jamie Berenger held their own press conference.

Jill Mayers, of ABC News, asked, "The president says you are heroes. Is that true?"

Jamie Berenger said, "We are ordinary men. We are not heroes. All of those who resisted the BATF are heroes."

Jane Rubenstein, of Newsweek, asked, "Are you concerned that the country will now become an armed camp and that we will be living in the Wild West and in fear for our lives?"

"I have heard this question asked in many different ways," Jesse Washington said. "I want you to listen to my answer. This whole thing was not about guns. It was about liberty. It was about freedom. You can't be free when the government breaks down your door instead of knocking."

Jamie Berenger said, "Guns are just tools. They are what you need to resist tyranny. Jesse, Aaron and I saw tyranny in Europe when we were young men. And the people there died because they had no guns. We didn't want that to happen here."

Jesse got up and took the microphone. "We're old men and we're tired, so you'll have to excuse us. But I have one more thing to say. We've now made peace with this government. It doesn't seem to be a tyrant. But freedom from tyrants is not something you can take for granted. It could come up again. And if it does, it will have to be resisted, just like it was this time.

"For you people out there who are younger than we are, it will fall to you to do the resisting next time. All we have done is preserve the opportunity for you to do that. We have buried the hatchet, but we have left the handle out where you can grab it."

With that, the old men shuffled off the stage, ignoring the questions that reporters were shouting at them. When it became clear that they would talk no more, the crowd cheered.

* * *

Sam and Gregory Naratova were walking along the Allegheny River trail on the north side of the river. Naratova wore his trench coat and ball cap. Sam wore a wool sweater and a boonie hat that had seen service in more than one remote part of the world.

"Would you have done it?" Naratova asked.

"What?"

"Shot the president if he had not resigned."

"Is that what I was supposed to do?" Sam said.

"You have a short memory."

"I did what I had to do."

"I know that. I'm asking you what you would have done if he had not resigned."